Kabumpo in Oz

Founded on and Continuing the Famous 'Oz'
Stories by L. Frank Baum
"Royal Historian of Oz"

Ruth Plumly Thompson

TABLE OF CONTENTS

This book is dedicated with all of my heart to Janet

My littlest sister but biggest assistor

Ruth Plumly Thompson

Dear Children:

Do you like Elephants? Do you believe in Giants? And do you love all the jolly people of the Wonderful Land of Oz?

Well, then you'll want to hear about the latest happenings in that delightful Kingdom. All are set forth in true Oz fashion in "Kabumpo in Oz," the fifteenth Oz book. Kabumpo is an Elegant Elephant. He is very old and wise, and has a kindly heart, as have all the Oz folks. In the new book you'll meet Prince Pompa, and Peg Amy, a charming Wooden Doll. There are new countries, strange adventures and the most surprising Box of Magic you have ever heard of. Ruggedo, the wicked old Gnome King, does a lot of mischief with this before Princess Ozma can stop him.

Of course Dorothy, the Scarecrow, Scraps, Glinda the Good, Tik-Tok, and other old friends all are alive and busy in the new book. I am just back from the Emerald City with the best of Oz wishes for everybody, *but especially for you.*

Ruth Plumly Thompson.
Philadelphia,
Spring of 1922

iv

Chapter 1
The Exploding Birthday Cake

"The cake, you chattering Chittimong! Where is the cake? Stirem, Friem, Hashem, *where* is the cake?" cried Eejabo, chief footman in the palace of Pumperdink, bouncing into the royal pantry.

The three cooks, too astonished for speech, and with staring eyes, pointed to the center table. The great, gorgeous birthday cake was gone, though not two seconds before it had been placed on the table by Hashem himself. "It was my m-m-asterpiece," sobbed Hashem, tearing off his cap and throwing his apron over his head.

"Help! Robbers! Thieves!" cried Stirem and Friem, running to the window.

Here *was* a howdedo. The trumpets blowing for the celebration to begin and the best part of the celebration gone!

"We'll all be dipped for this!" wailed Eejabo, flinging open the second best china closet so violently that three silver cups and a pewter mug tumbled out. Just then there was a scream from Hashem, who had removed the apron from his head. "Look!" he shrieked. "There it is!"

Back to the table rushed the other three, Stirem and Friem rubbing their eyes and Eejabo his head where the cups had bumped him severely. Upon the table stood the royal cake, as pink and perfect as ever.

"It was there all the time, mince my eyebrows!" spluttered Hashem in an injured voice. "Called me a Chittimong, did you?" Grasping a big wooden spoon he ran angrily at Eejabo. "Was it gone or wasn't it?" cried Eejabo, appealing to the others and hastily catching up a bread knife to defend himself. Instantly there arose a babble.

"It was!"

"It wasn't!"

"Was!" Rap, bang, *clatter*. In a minute they were in a furious argument, not only with words but with spoons, forks and bowls. And dear knows what would have become of the cake had not a bell rung loudly and the second footman poked his head through the door.

"The cake! Where is the cake?" he wheezed importantly.

So Eejabo, dodging three cups and a salt cellar, seized the great silver platter and dashed into the great banquet hall. One pink coat tail was missing and his wig was

1

somewhat elevated over the left ear from the lump raised by the pewter mug, but he summoned what dignity he could and joined the grand procession of footmen who were bearing gold and silver dishes filled with goodies for the birthday feast of Prince Pompadore of Pumperdink.

The royal guests were already assembled and just as Eejabo entered, the pages blew a shrill blast upon their silver trumpets and the Prime Pumper stepped forward to announce their Majesties.

"Oyez! Oyez!" shouted the Prime Pumper, pounding on the floor with his silver staff, while the guests politely inclined their heads just as if they had not heard the same announcement dozens of times before:

"Oyez! Oyez!
"Pompus the Proud
And Pozy Pink,
King and Queen
Of Pumperdink—
Way for the King
And clear the floor,
Way for our good
Prince Pompadore.
Way for the Elegant
Elephant—Way
For the King and
The Queen and the
Prince, I say!"

So everybody *wayed*, which is to say they bowed, and down the center of the room swept Pompus, very fat and gorgeous in his purple robes and jeweled crown, and Pozy Pink, very stately and queenlike in her ermine cloak, and Prince Pompadore very straight and handsome! In fact, they looked exactly as a good old-fashioned royal family should.

Pumperdink

But Kabumpo, who swayed along grandly after the Prince—few royal families could boast of so royal and elegant an elephant! He was huge and gray. On his head he wore jeweled bands and a jeweled court robe billowed out majestically as he walked.

2

His little eyes twinkled merrily and his big ears flapped so sociably, that just to look at him put one in a good humor. Kabumpo was the only elephant in Pumperdink, or in any Kingdom near Pumperdink, so no wonder he was a prime favorite at Court. He had been given to the King at Pompa's christening by a friendly stranger and since then had enjoyed every luxury and advantage. He was not only treated as a member of the royal family, but was always addressed as *Sir* by all of the palace servants.

"He lends an air of elegance to our Court," the King was fond of saying, and the Elegant Elephant he surely had become. Now an Elegant Elephant at Court might seem strange in a regular up-to-date country, but Pumperdink is not at all regular nor up to date. It is a cozy, old-fashioned Kingdom, 'way up in the northern part of the Gilliken country of Oz; old-fashioned enough to wear knee breeches and have a King and cozy enough to still enjoy birthday parties and candy pulls.

If Pompus, the King, was a bit proud who could blame him? His Queen was the loveliest, his son the most charming and his elephant the most elegant and unusual for twenty Kingdoms round about. And Pompus, for all his pride, had a very simple way of ruling. When the Pumperdinkians did right they were rewarded; when they did wrong they were dipped.

In the very center of the courtyard there is a great stone well with a huge stone bucket. Into this Pumperdink well all offenders and law breakers were lowered. Its waters were dark blue and as the color stuck to one for several days the inhabitants of Pumperdink were careful to behave well, so that the Chief Dipper, who turned the wheel that raised and lowered the bucket, often had days at a time with nothing to do. This time he spent in writing poetry, and as Prince Pompadore took the place of honor at the head of the table the Chief Dipper rose from his humble place at the foot and with a moist flourish burst forth:

"Oh, Pompadore of Pumperdink,
Of all perfection you're the pink;
Your praises now I utter!
Your eyes are clear as apple sauce,
Your head the best I've come across;
Your heart is soft as butter."

"Very good," said the King, and the Chief Dipper sat down, blushing with pride and confusion. Prince Pompadore bowed and the rest of the party clapped tremendously. "Sounds like a dipper full of nonsense to me," wheezed Kabumpo, who stood directly back of Prince Pompadore's throne, leisurely consuming a bale of hay placed on the floor beside him. It may surprise you to know that all the animals in Oz can talk, but such is the case, and Pumperdink being in the fairy country of Oz, Kabumpo could talk as well as my man and better than most.

"Eyes like apple sauce—heart of butter! Ho-ho, kerrumph!" The Elegant Elephant laughed so hard he shook all over; then slyly reaching over the Prime Pumper's shoulder, he snatched his glass of pink lemonade and emptied it down his great throat, setting the tumbler back before the old fellow turned his head.

"Did you call, Sir?" asked Eejabo, hurrying over. He had mistaken Kabumpo's laugh for a command.

"Yes; why did you not give his Excellency lemonade?" demanded the Elegant Elephant sternly.

"I did; he must have drunk it, Sir!" stuttered Eejabo.

"Drunk it!" cried the Prime Pumper, pounding on the table indignantly. "I never had any!"

3

"Fetch him a glass at once," rumbled Kabumpo, waving his trunk, and Eejabo, too wise to argue with a member of the royal family, brought another glass of lemonade. But no sooner had he done so than the mischievous elephant stole that, next the Prime Pumper's plate and roll, and all so quickly, no one but Prince Pompadore knew what was happening and poor Eejabo was kept running backwards and forwards till his wig stood on end with confusion and rage.

All of this was very amusing to the Prince, and helped him to listen pleasantly to the fifteen long birthday speeches addressed to him by members of the Royal Guard. But if the speeches were dull, the dinner was not. The fiddlers fiddled so merrily, and the chief cook Hashem had so outdone himself in the preparation of new and delicious dainties, that by ice-cream-and-cake time everyone was in a high good humor.

"The cake, my good Eejabo! Fetch forth the cake!" commanded King Pompus, beaming fondly upon his son. Nervously Eejabo stepped to the side table and lighted the eighteen tall birthday candles. A cake that had disappeared once might easily do so again, and Eejabo was anxious to have it cut and out of the way—out of *his* way at least.

Hashem, looking through a tiny crack in the door, almost burst with pride as his gorgeous pink masterpiece was set down before the Prince.

"Many happy returns of your eighteenth birthday!" cried the Courtiers, jumping to their feet and waving their napkins enthusiastically.

"Thank you! Thank you!" chuckled Pompadore, bowing low. "I feel that this is but one of many more to come!" Which may sound strange, but Pumperdink being in Oz, one may have as many eighteenth birthdays as one cares to have. This was Pompa's tenth and while the courtiers drank his health the Prince made ready to blow out the birthday candles.

"That's right, blow 'em all out at once!" cried the King. So Pompa puffed out his cheeks and blew with all his might. But not a candle flickered. Then he tried again. Indeed, he puffed and blew until he was a regular royal purple, but nary a candle flame so much as wavered.

"Stubbornest candles I ever saw!" blustered King Pompus. Then *he* puffed out his cheeks and blew like a porpoise; so did Queen Pozy and the Prime Pumper; so did everybody. They blew until every dish upon the table skipped and they all sank back exhausted in their chairs, but the candles burned as merrily as ever.

Then Kabumpo took a hand—or rather a trunk. He had been watching the proceedings with his twinkling little eyes. Now he took a tremendous breath, pointed his trunk straight at the cake and blew with all his strength.

Every candle went out—but *stars*! As they did, the great pink cake exploded with such force that half the Courtiers were flung under the table and the rest knocked unconscious by flying fragments of icing, tumblers and plates.

"*Treason!*" screamed Pompus, the first to recover from the shock. "Who dared put gunpowder in the cake?" Brushing the icing from his nose, he glared around angrily. The first person to catch his eye was Hashem, the cook, who stood trembling in the doorway.

"*Dip him!*" shouted the King furiously. And the Chief Dipper, only too glad of an excuse to escape, seized poor Hashem. "*And him!*" ordered the King, as Eejabo tried to sidle out of the room. "*And them!*" as all the other footmen started to run. Forming his victims in a line the Chief Dipper marched them sternly from the banquet hall.

"Oyez! Oyez Everybody shall be dipped!" mumbled the Prime Pumper, feebly raising his head.

"Oh, no! Oh, no! Nothing of the sort!" snapped the King, fanning poor Queen Pozy Pink with a plate. She had fainted dead away.

"What is the meaning of this outrage?" shouted Pompus, his anger rising again.

"How should I know?" wheezed Kabumpo, dragging Prince Pompadore from beneath the table and pouring a jug of cream over his head.

"Something hit me," moaned the Prince, opening his eyes.

"Of course it did!" said Kabumpo. "The cake hit you. Made a great hit with us all—that cake!" The Elegant Elephant looked ruefully at his silk robe of state, which was hopelessly smeared with icing; then put his trunk to his head, for something hard had struck him between the eyes. He felt about the floor and found a round shiny object which he was about to show the King when Pompus pounced upon a tall scroll sitting upright in his tumbler. In the confusion of the moment it had escaped his attention.

"Perhaps this will explain," spluttered the King, breaking the seal. Queen Pozy Pink opened her eyes with a sigh, and the Courtiers, crawling out from beneath the table, looked up anxiously, for everyone was still dazed from the tremendous explosion. Pompus read the scroll to himself with popping eyes and then began to dance up and down in a frenzy.

"What is it? What is it?" cried the Queen, trying to read over his shoulder. Then she gave a well-bred scream and fainted away in the arms of General Quakes, who had come up behind her.

By this time the Prime Pumper had recovered sufficiently to remember that reading scrolls and court papers was his business. Somewhat unsteadily he walked over and took the scroll from the King.

"Oyez! Oyez!" he faltered, pounding on the table.

"Oh, never mind that!" rumbled Kabumpo, flagging his ears. "Let's hear what it says!"

"Know ye," began the old man in a high, shaky voice, "know ye that unless ye Prince of ye ancient and honorable Kingdom of Pumperdink wed ye Proper Fairy Princess in ye proper span of time ye Kingdom of Pumperdink shall disappear forever and *even longer* from ye Gilliken country of Oz.

J. G."

"What?" screamed Pompadore, bounding to his feet. "Me? But I don't *want* to marry!"

"You'll have to," groaned the King, with a wave at the scroll. The Courtiers sat staring at one another in dazed disbelief. From the courtyard came the splash and splutter of the luckless footmen and the dismal creaking of the stone bucket.

"Oh!" wailed Pompa, throwing up his hands. "This is the worst eighteenth birthday I've ever had. I'll never have another as long as I live!"

Chapter 2
Picking a Proper Princess

"What shall we do first?" groaned the King, holding his head with both hands. "Let me think!"

"Right," said Kabumpo. "Think by all means."

So the great hall was cleared and the King, with the mysterious scroll spread out before him, thought and thought and *thought*. But he did not make much

31

headway, for, as he explained over and over to Queen Pozy, who—with Pompadore, the Elegant Elephant and the Prime Pumper—had remained to help him, "How is one to know where to find the Proper Princess, and how is one to know the proper time for Pompa to wed her?"

Who was J.G.? How did the scroll get in the cake?

The more the King thought about these questions, the more wrinkled his forehead became.

"Why! We're liable to wake up any morning and find ourselves gone," he announced gloomily. "How does it feel to disappear, I wonder?"

"I suppose it would give one rather a gone feeling, but I don't believe it would hurt—much!" volunteered Kabumpo, glancing uneasily over his shoulder.

"Perhaps not, but it would not get us anywhere. My idea is to marry the Prince at once to a Proper Princess," put in the Prime Pumper, "and avoid all this disappearing."

"You're in a great hurry to marry me off, aren't you," said Pompadore sulkily. "For my part, I don't want to marry at all!"

"Well, that's very selfish of you, Pompa," said the King in a grieved voice. "Do you want your poor old father to disappear?"

"Not only your poor old father," choked the Prime Pumper, rolling up his eyes. "How about me?"

"Oh, you—*you* can disappear any time you want," said the Prince unfeelingly.

"It all started with that wretched cake," sighed the Queen. "I am positive the scroll flew out of the cake when it exploded."

"Of course it did!" cried Pompus. "Let us send for the cook and question him."

So Hashem, very wet and blue from his dip, was brought before the King.

"A fine cook you are!" roared Pompus, "mixing gun powder and scrolls in a birthday cake."

"But I didn't," wailed Hashem, falling on his knees. "Only eggs, your Highness— very best eggs—sugar, flour, spice and—"

"Bombshells!" cried the King angrily.

"The cake disappeared *before* the party, your Majesty!" cried Eejabo.

Everyone jumped at the sudden interruption, and Eejabo, who had crept in unnoticed, stepped before the throne.

"Disappeared," continued Eejabo hoarsely, dripping blue water all over the royal rugs. "One minute there it was on the pantry table. Next minute—*gone!*" croaked Eejabo, flinging up his hands and shrugging his shoulders.

"Then, before a fellow could turn around, it was back. 'Tweren't our fault if magic got mixed into it, and here we have been dipped for nothing!"

"Well, why didn't you say so before!" asked the King in exasperation.

"Fine chance I had to say anything!" sniffed Eejabo, wringing out his lace ruffles.

"Eh—rr—you may have the day off, my good man," said Pompus, with an apologetic cough—"And *you* also," with a wave at Hashem. Very stiffly the two walked to the door.

"It's an off day for us, all right," said Eejabo ungraciously, and without so much as a bow the two disappeared.

"I fear you were a bit hasty, my love," murmured Queen Pozy, looking after them with a troubled little frown.

"Well, who wouldn't be!" cried Pompus, ruffling up his hair. "Here we are liable to disappear any minute and all you do is to stand around and criticize me. *Begone!*" he puffed angrily, as a page stuck his head in the door.

"No use shouting at people to begone," said the Elegant Elephant testily. "We'll all begone soon enough."

At this Queen Pozy began to weep into her silk handkerchief, which sight so affected Prince Pompadore that he rushed forward and embraced her tenderly.

"I'll marry!" cried the Prince impulsively. "I'll do anything! The trouble is there aren't any Fairy Princesses around here!"

"There must be," said the King.

"There is—There are!" screamed the Prime Pumper, bouncing up suddenly. "Oyez, Oyez! Has your Majesty forgotten Faleero, royal Princess of Follensby forest?"

"Why, of course!" The King snapped his fingers joyfully. "Everyone says Faleero is a Fairy Princess. She must be the proper one!"

"Fa—*leero!*" trumpeted the Elegant Elephant, sitting down with a terrific thud. "That awful old creature! You ought to be ashamed of yourself!"

"Silence!" thundered the King.

"Nonsense!" trumpeted Kabumpo. "She's a thousand years old and as ugly as a stone Lukoogoo. Don't you marry her, Pompa."

"I command him to marry her!" cried the King opening his eyes very wide and bending forward.

"Faleero?" gasped the Prince, scarcely believing his ears. No wonder Pompadore was shocked. Faleero, although a Princess in her own right and of royal fairy descent, was so unattractive that in all her thousand years of life no one had wished to marry her. She lived in a small hut in the great forest kingdom next to Pumperdink and did nothing all day but gather faggots. Her face was long and lean, her hair thin and black and her nose so large that it made you think of a cauliflower.

"Ugh!" groaned Prince Pompadore, falling back on Kabumpo for support.

"Well, she's a Princess and a fairy—the only one in any Kingdom. I don't see why you want to be so fussy!" said the King fretfully.

"Shall I tell her Royal Highness of the great good fortune that has befallen her?" asked the Prime Pumper, starting for the door.

"Do so at once," snapped Pompus. Just then he gave a scream of fright and pain, for a round shiny object had flown through the air and struck him on the head. "What was that?"

The Prime Pumper looked suspiciously at the Elegant Elephant. Kabumpo glared back.

"A—a warning!" stuttered the Prime Pumper, afraid to say that Kabumpo had flung the offending missile. "A warning, your Majesty!"

"It's nothing of the kind," said the King angrily. "You're getting old, Pumper and stupid. It's—why it's a door knob! Who *dares* to hit me with a door knob?"

"It hit me once," mumbled Kabumpo, shifting uneasily from one foot to the other three. "How does it strike you?"

"As an outrageous piece of impertinence!" spluttered Pompus, turning as red as a turkey cock.

"Perhaps it has something to do with the scroll," suggested Queen Pozy, taking it from the King. "See! It is gold and all the door knobs in the palace are ivory. And look! Here are some initials!"

Sure enough! It was gold and in the very centre were the initials P. A.

Just at this interesting juncture the page, who had been poking his head in the door every few minutes, gathered his courage together and rushed up to the King.

"Pardon, Most High Highness, but General Quakes bade me say that this mirror was found under the window," stuttered the page, and before Pompus had an opportunity to cry "Begone!" or "Dip him!" the little fellow made a dash for the door and disappeared.

"It grows more puzzling every minute," wailed the King, looking from the door knob to the mirror and from the mirror to the scroll.

"If you take my advice you'll have this marriage performed at once," said the Prime Pumper in a trembling voice.

"I believe I will!" sighed Pompus, rubbing the bump on his head. "Go and fetch the Princess Faleero and you, Pompa, prepare for your wedding."

"But Father!" began the Prince.

"Not another word or you'll be dipped!" rumbled the King of Pumperdink. "I'm not going to have my kingdom disappearing if I can help it!"

"You mean if *I* can help it," muttered Pompadore gloomily.

"This is ridiculous!" stormed the Elegant Elephant, as the Prime Pumper rushed importantly out of the room. "Don't you know that this country of ours is only a small part of the great Kingdom of Oz? There must be hundreds of Princesses for Pompadore to choose from. Why should he not wed Ozma, the princess of us all? Haven't you read any Oz history? Have you never heard of the wonderful Emerald City? Let Pompadore start out at once. I, myself, will accompany him, and if Ozma refuses to marry him—well"—the Elegant Elephant drew himself up—"I will carry her off—that's all!"

"It's a long way to the Emerald City," mused Queen Pozy, "but still—"

"Yes, and what is to become of us in the meantime pray? While you are wandering all over Oz we can disappear I suppose! No Sir! Not one step do you go out of Pumperdink. Faleero is the Proper Princess and Pompadore shall marry her!" said Pompus.

"You're talking through your crown," wheezed Kabumpo. "How about the door knob and mirror? They came out of the cake as well as the scroll. What are you going to do about them? Let's have a look at that mirror."

"Just a common gold mirror," fumed Pompus, holding it up for the Elegant Elephant to see.

"What's the matter?" as Kabumpo gave a snort.

On the face of the mirror, as Kabumpo looked in, two words appeared:

Elegant Elephant.

And when Pompus snatched the mirror, above his reflection stood the words:

Fat Old King.

Then Queen Pozy peeped into the mirror, which promptly flashed:

Lovely Queen.

"Why, it's telling the truth!" screamed Pompa, looking over his mother's shoulder. At this the words "Charming Prince" formed quickly in the glass.

The Prince grinned at his father, who was now quite beside himself with rage.

"You think I'm fat and old, do you!" snorted the King, flinging the gold mirror face down on the table. "This is a nice day, I must say! Scrolls, door knobs, mirrors and insults!"

"But what can P. A. stand for?" mused Queen Pozy thoughtfully.

"Plain enough," chuckled Kabumpo, maliciously. "It stands for perfectly awful!"

"Who's perfectly awful?" asked Pompus suspiciously.

"Why, Faleero," sniffed the Elegant Elephant. "That's plain enough to everybody!"

"Dip him!" shrieked Pompus. "I've had enough of this! *Dip him*—do you hear?"

"That," yawned Kabumpo, straightening his silk robe, "is impossible!" And, considering his size it was. But just that minute the Prime Pumper returned and in his interest to hear what the Princess Faleero had said the King forgot about dipping Kabumpo.

The courier from the Princess stepped forward.

"Her Highness," puffed the Prime Pumper, who had run all the way, "Her Highness accepts Prince Pompadore with pleasure and will marry him to-morrow morning."

Prince Pompadore gave a dismal groan.

"Fine!" cried the King, rubbing his hands together. "Let everything be made ready for the ceremony, and in the meantime"—Pompus glared about fiercely—"I forbid anyone's disappearing. I am still the King! Set a guard around the castle, Pumper, to watch for any signs of disappearance, and if so much as a fence paling disappears"— he drew himself up—"notify me *at once!*" Then turning to the throne Pompus gave his arm to Queen Pozy and together they started for the garden.

"Do you mean to say you are going to pay no attention to the mirror or door knob?" cried Kabumpo, planting himself in the King's path.

"Go away," said Pompus crossly.

"Oyez! Oyez! Way for their Majesties!" cried the Prime Pumper, running ahead with his silver staff, and the royal couple swept out of the banquet hall.

"Never mind, Kabumpo," said the Prince, flinging his arm affectionately around the Elegant Elephant's trunk, "I dare say Faleero has her good points—and we cannot let the old Kingdom disappear, you know!"

"Flinging his arms affectionately around the Elegant Elephant's trunk"

"Fiddlesticks!" choked Kabumpo. "She'll make a door mat of you, Pompa—Prince Pompadormat—that's what you'll be! Let's run away!" he proposed, his little eyes twinkling anxiously.

"I couldn't do that and let the Kingdom disappear, it wouldn't be right," sighed the Prince, and sadly he followed his parents into the royal gardens.

"The King's a Gooch!" gulped the Elegant Elephant unhappily. Then, all at once he flung up his trunk. "Somebody's going to disappear around here," he wheezed darkly, "that's certain!" With a mighty rustling of his silk robe, Kabumpo hurried off to his own royal quarters in the palace.

Left alone, Prince Pompa threw himself down at the foot of the throne, and gazed sadly into space.

Chapter 3
Kabumpo and Pompa Disappear

Once in his own apartment, Kabumpo pulled the bell rope furiously.

"My pearls and my purple plush robe! Bring them at once!" he puffed when his personal attendant appeared in the doorway.

"Yes, Sir! Are you going out, Sir?" murmured the little Pumperdinkian, hastening to a great chest in the corner of the big marble room, to get out of the robe.

"Not unless disappearing is going out," said Kabumpo more mildly, for he was quite fond of this little man who waited on him. "But I'm liable to disappear any minute. So are you. So is everybody, and I, for my part, wish to do the thing well and disappear with as much elegance as possible. Have you heard about the magic scroll, Spezzle?"

"Yes, Sir!" quavered Spezzle, mounting a ladder to adjust the Elegant Elephant's pearls and gorgeous robe of state. "Yes, Sir, and my head's going round and round like—"

"Like what?" asked Kabumpo, looking approvingly at his reflection in the long mirror.

"I can't rightly say, Sir," sighed Spezzle. "This disappearing has me that mixed up I don't know what I'm doing."

"Well, don't start by losing your head," chuckled Kabumpo. "There—that will do very well." He lifted the little man down from the ladder. "Good-bye, Spezzle. If you should disappear before I should see you again, try to do it in style."

"Yes, Sir!" gulped Spezzle. Then taking out a bright red handkerchief he blew his nose violently and rushed out of the room. Kabumpo walked up and down before the mirror, surveying himself from all angles. A very gorgeous appearance he presented, in his purple plush robe of state, all embroidered in silver, and his head bands of shining pearls. In the left side of his robe there was a deep pocket. Into this the Elegant Elephant slipped all the jewels he possessed, taking them from a drawer in the chest.

"I must get that gold door knob," he rumbled thoughtfully. "And the mirror." Noiselessly (for all his tremendous size, Kabumpo could move without a sound) he made his way back to the banquet hall and loomed up suddenly behind the Prime Pumper. The old fellow was staring with popping eyes into the gold mirror.

"Ho, Ho!" roared Kabumpo. "Ho, Ho! Kerumph!"

No wonder! Above the shocked reflection of the foolish statesman stood the words "Old Goose!"

"A truthful mirror, indeed," wheezed the Elegant Elephant.

"Heh? What?" stuttered the Prime Pumper, slapping the mirror down on the table in a hurry. "Where'd you come from? What are you all dressed up for?"

"For my disappearance," said Kabumpo, sweeping the door knob and mirror into his pocket. "I'm getting ready to disappear. How do I look?"

Before the Prime Pumper had time to answer, the Elegant Elephant was gone.

Back in his own room, Kabumpo paced impatiently up and down, waiting for night. "I do not see how she could refuse us," he mumbled every now and then to himself.

That was an anxious afternoon and evening in the palace of Pumperdink. Every few minutes the Courtiers felt themselves nervously to see if they were still there. The servants went about on tip-toe, looking fearfully over their shoulders for the first signs of disappearance. As it grew darker the gates and windows were securely barred and not a candle was lighted. "The less the castle shows, the less likely it is to disappear," reasoned the King.

The darkness suited Kabumpo. He waited until everyone in the palace had retired, and a full hour longer. Then he stepped softly down the passage to the Prince's apartment. Pompadore, without undressing had flung himself upon a couch and fallen into an uneasy slumber.

Without making a sound, Kabumpo took the Prince's crown from a dressing cabinet, slipped it carefully into the pocket of his robe, and then carefully lifted the sleeping Prince in his curling trunk and started cautiously down the great hall. Setting him gently on the floor as he reached the palace doors, he pushed back the golden bolts and stepped out into the garden.

The voices of the watchmen calling to each other from the great wall came faintly through the darkness, but the Elegant Elephant hurried to a secret unguarded entrance known only to himself and Pompadore and passed like a great shadow through the swinging gates. Once outside, he swung the sleeping Prince to his broad back and ran swiftly and silently through the night.

"What are we doing?" murmured the Prince drowsily in his sleep.

"Disappearing," chuckled Kabumpo under his breath. "Disappearing from Pumperdink, my lad."

Chapter 4
The Curious Cottabus Appears

"Ouch!" Prince Pompadore stirred uneasily and rolled over. "Ouch!" he groaned again, giving his pillow a fretful thump. "Ouch!" This time his eyes flew wide open, for his knuckles were tingling with pain.

"A rock!" gasped the Prince, sitting up indignantly. "A rock under my head! No wonder it aches! Great Gillikens! Where am I?" He stared about wildly. There was not a familiar object in sight. Indeed he was in a dim, deep forest, and from the distance came the sound of someone sawing wood.

"Oh! Oh! I know!" muttered the Prince, rubbing his head miserably. "It's that wretched scroll. I've disappeared and this is the place I've disappeared to." Stiffly he

13

got to his feet and started to walk in the direction of the sawing, but had only gone a few steps before he gave a cry of joy, for there, leaning up against a tree, snoring like twenty wood-cutters at work, was Kabumpo.

"Wake up!" cried Pompadore, pounding him with all his might. "Wake up, Kabumpo. We've disappeared!"

"Have we?" yawned the Elegant Elephant, opening one eye. "You don't say? Hah, Hoh, Hum!" With a tremendous yawn he opened the other eye and began to chuckle and shake all over.

"We stole a march on 'em, Pompa. I'd like to see the King's face when he finds us gone. Old Pumper will be Oyezing all over the palace. He'll think we've disappeared by magic."

"Well, didn't we?" asked Pompadore in amazement.

"Not unless you call *me* magic. I carried you off in the night. Did you suppose old Kabumpo was going to stand quietly by while they married you to a faggotty old fairy like Faleero? Not much," wheezed the Elegant Elephant. "I have other plans for you, little one!"

"But this is terrible!" cried the Prince, catching hold of a tree. "Here you have left my poor old father, my lovely mother, and the whole Kingdom of Pumperdink to disappear. We'll have to go right straight back—right straight back to Pumperdink. Do you hear?"

"Do have a little sense!" Kabumpo shook himself crossly. "You can't save them by going back. The thing to do is to go forward, find the Proper Princess and marry her. No scroll magic takes effect for seven days, anyway!"

"How do you know?" asked Pompa anxiously.

"Read it in a witch book," answered Kabumpo promptly. "Now, that gives us plenty of time to go to the Emerald City and present ourselves to the lovely ruler of Oz. There's a Proper Princess for you, Pompa!"

"But suppose she refuses me," said the Prince uncertainly.

"You're very handsome, Pompa, my boy." The Elegant Elephant gave the Prince a playful poke with his trunk. "I've brought all my jewels as gifts and the magic mirror and door knob as well. If she refuses you and the worst comes to the worst"— Kabumpo cleared his throat gravely—"well—just leave it to me!"

After a bit more coaxing and after eating the breakfast Kabumpo had thoughtfully brought along, Pompa allowed the Elegant Elephant to lift him on his head and off they set at Kabumpo's best speed for the Emerald City of Oz.

Neither the Prince nor the Elegant Elephant had ever been out of Pumperdink, but Kabumpo had found an old map of Oz in the palace library. According to this map, the Emerald City lay directly to the South of their own country. "So all we have to do is to keep going South," chuckled Kabumpo softly. Pompadore nodded, but he was trying to recall the exact words of the mysterious scroll:

"Know Ye, that unless ye Prince of ye ancient and honorable Kingdom of Pumperdink shall wed ye Proper Fairy Princess in ye proper span of time ye Kingdom of Pumperdink shall disappear forever and even longer from ye Gilliken Country of Oz. *J. G.*"

Pompadore repeated the words solemnly; then fell a-thinking of all he had heard of Ozma of Oz, the loveliest little fairy imaginable.

"She wouldn't want one of her Kingdom to disappear," reflected Pompadore sagely.

Now, as it happened, Ozma did not even know of the existence of Pumperdink. Oz is so large and inhabited by so many strange and singular peoples that although fourteen books of history have been written about it, only half the story has been told. There are no Oz railway or steamship lines and traveling is tedious and slow, owing to the magic nature of the land itself, its many mountains and fairy forests, so that Pumperdink, like many of the small Kingdoms on the outskirts of Oz, has never been explored by Ozma.

Oz itself is a huge oblong country divided into four parts, the North being the purple Gilliken country, the East the blue Munchkin country, the South the red lands of the Quadlings, and the West the pleasant yellow country of the Winkies. In the very center of Oz, as almost every boy and girl knows, is the wonderful Emerald City, and in its gorgeous green palace lives Ozma, the lovely little Fairy Princess, whom Kabumpo wanted Pompadore to marry.

"Do you know," mused the Prince, after they had traveled some time through the dim forest, "I believe that gold mirror has a lot to do with all this. I believe it was put in the cake to help me find the Proper Princess."

"Where would you find a more Proper Princess than Ozma?" puffed Kabumpo indignantly. "Ozma is the one—depend upon it!"

"Just the same," said Pompa firmly, "I'm going to try every Princess we meet!"

"Do you expect to find 'em running wild in the woods?" snorted Kabumpo, who didn't like to be contradicted.

"You never can tell." The Prince of Pumperdink settled back comfortably. Now that they were really started, he was finding traveling extremely interesting. "I should have done this long ago," murmured the Prince to himself. "Every Prince should go on a journey of adventure."

"How long will it take us to reach the Emerald City?" he asked presently.

"Two days, if nothing happens," answered Kabumpo. "Say—what's that?" He stopped short and spread his ears till they looked like sails. The underbrush at the right was crackling from the springs of some large animal, and next minute a hoarse voice roared:

"I want to know
The which and what,
The where and how and why?
A curious, luxurious
Old Cottabus am I!
I want to know the
When and who,
The whatfor and whyso, Sir!
So please attend, there is no end
To things I want to know, Sir!"

"Aha!" exulted the voice triumphantly. "There you are!" And a great round head was thrust out, almost in Kabumpo's face. "Oh! I'm going to enjoy this. Don't move!"

Kabumpo was too astonished to move, and the next instant the Cottabus had flounced out of the bushes and settled itself directly in front of the two travelers. It was large as a pony, but shaped like a great overfed cat. Its eyes bulged unpleasantly and the end of its tail ended in a large fan.

The Cottabus was as large as a pony, but shaped like a great overfed cat

"Well," grunted Kabumpo after the strange creature had regarded them for a full minute without blinking.

"Well, what?" it asked, beginning to fan itself sulkily. "You act as if you had never seen a Cottabus before."

"We never have," admitted Pompa, peering over Kabumpo's head and secretly wishing he had brought along his jeweled sword.

"Why haven't you?" asked the Cottabus, rolling up its eyes. "How frightfully ignorant!" It closed its fan tail with a snap and looked up at them disapprovingly. "Will you kindly tell me who you are, where you came from, when you came, what you are going for, how you are going to get it, why you are going and what you are going to do when you do get it!"

"I don't see why we should tell you all that," grumbled Kabumpo. "Its none of your affair."

"Wrong!" shrieked the creature hysterically. "It is the business of a Cottabus to find out everything. I live on other people's affairs, and unless"—here it paused, took a large handkerchief out of a pocket in its fur and began to wipe its eyes—"unless a Cottabus asks fifty questions a day it curls up in its porch rocker and d-d-dies, and this is my fifth questionless day."

"Curl up and die, then," said Kabumpo gruffly. But the kind-hearted Prince felt sorry for the foolish creature.

"If we answer your questions, will you answer ours?"

"I'll try," sniffed the Curious Cottabus, and leaning over it dragged a rocking chair out of the bushes and seated itself comfortably.

"Well, then," began Pompa, "this is the Elegant Elephant and I am a Prince. We came from Pumperdink because our Kingdom was threatened with disappearance unless I marry a Proper Princess."

16

"Yes," murmured the Cottabus, rocking violently. "Yes, yes!"

"And we are going to the Emerald City to ask Princess Ozma for her hand," continued the Prince.

"How do you know she is the one? When did this happen? Who brought the message? What are you going to do if Ozma refuses you?" asked the Cottabus, leaning forward breathlessly.

"Are you going to stand talking to this ridiculous creature all day?" grumbled Kabumpo. But Pompadore, perhaps because he was so young, felt flattered that even a curious old Cottabus should take such an interest in his affairs. So beginning at the very beginning he told the whole story of his birthday party.

"Yes, yes," gulped the Cottabus wildly each time the Prince paused for breath. "Yes, yes," fluttering its fan excitedly. When Pompadore had finished the Cottabus leaned back, closed its eyes and put both paws on the arms of the rocker. "I never heard anything more curious in my life," said the curious one. "This will keep me amused for three days!"

"Of course—that's what we're here for—to amuse you!" said Kabumpo scornfully. "Lets be going, Pompa!"

"Perhaps the Curious Cottabus can tell us something of the country ahead. Are there any Princesses living 'round here?" the Prince asked eagerly.

"Never heard of any," said the Cottabus, opening its eyes. "Can you multiply—add—divide and subtract? Are you good at fractions, Prince?"

"Not very," admitted Pompadore, looking mystified.

"Then you won't make much headway," sighed the Cottabus, shaking its head solemnly. "Now, don't ask me why," it added lugubriously, dragging its rocker back into the brush, and while Kabumpo and Pompa stared in amazement it wriggled away into the bushes.

"Come on," cried Kabumpo with a contemptuous grunt, but he had only gone a few steps when the Curious Cottabus stuck its head out of an opening in the trees just ahead. "When are you coming back?" it asked, twitching its nose anxiously.

"Never!" trumpeted Kabumpo, increasing his speed. Again the Cottabus disappeared, only to reappear at the first turn in the road.

"Did you say the door knob hit you on the head?" it asked pleadingly.

Kabumpo gave a snort of anger and rushed along so fast that Pompa had to hang on for dear life.

"Guess we've left him behind this time," spluttered the Elegant Elephant, after he had run almost a mile.

But at that minute there was a wheeze from the underbrush and the head of the Cottabus was thrust out. Its tongue was hanging out and it was panting with exhaustion. "How old are you?" it gasped rolling its eyes pitifully. "Who was your grandfather on your father's side, and was he bald?"

"Kerumberty Bumpus!" raged the Elegant Elephant, flouncing to the other side of the road.

"But why was the door knob in the cake?" gulped the Cottabus, two tears trickling off its nose.

"How should we know," said Pompa coldly.

"Then just tell me the date of your birth," wailed the Cottabus, two tears trickling off its nose.

"No! No!" screamed Kabumpo, and this time he ran so fast that the tearful voice of the Cottabus became fainter and fainter and finally died away altogether.

"Provokingest creature I've ever met," grumbled the Elegant Elephant, and this time Pompa agreed with him.

"Isn't it almost lunch time?" asked the Prince. He was beginning to feel terribly hungry.

"And aren't there any villages or cities between here and the Emerald City?" Pompa spoke again.

"Don't know," wheezed Kabumpo, swinging ahead.

"Oh! There's a flag!" cried Pompa suddenly. "It's flying above the tree tops just ahead."

And so it was—a huge, flapping black flag covered with hundreds of figures and signs.

"Hurry up, Kabumpo," urged the Prince. "This looks interesting."

Chapter 5
In The City of The Figure Heads

"It reminds me of something disagreeable," answered Kabumpo, as he eyed the flag. Nevertheless he quickened his steps and in a moment they came to a clearing in the forest, surrounded by a tall black picket fence. The only thing visible above the fence was the strange black flag, and as the forest on either side was too dense to penetrate and there seemed to be no way around, Kabumpo thumped loudly on the center gate.

It was flung open at once, so suddenly that Kabumpo, who had his head pressed against the bars, fell on his knees and shot Pompadore clear over his head. Altogether it was a very undignified entrance.

"Oh! Oh! Now we shall have some fun!" screamed a high, thin voice, and immediately the cry was taken up by hundreds of other voices. A perfect swarm of strange creatures surrounded the two travelers. The Elegant Elephant took one look, put back his ears and snatched Pompa from the paving stones.

"Stop that!" he rumbled threateningly. "Who are you anyway?" The crowd paid no attention to the Elegant Elephant's question, but continued to dance up and down and scream with glee. Clutching Kabumpo's ear, Pompa peered down with many misgivings. They were entirely surrounded by thin, spry little people, who had figures instead of heads, and the fours, eights, sevens and ciphers bobbing up and down made it terribly confusing.

"Let's go!" said Pompa, who was growing dizzier every minute. But the Figure Heads were wedged so closely around them Kabumpo could not move and they were shouting so lustily that the Elegant Elephant's voice was drowned in the hubbub. Finally, Kabumpo's eyes began to snap angrily and, taking a deep breath, he threw up his trunk and trumpeted like fifty ferry-boat whistles. The effect was immediate and astonishing. Half of the Figure Heads fell on their faces, and the other half fell on their backs and stared vacantly up at the sky.

"Conduct us to your Ruler!" roared Kabumpo, in the dead silence that followed.

"How'd you know we had a Ruler?" asked a Seven, getting cautiously to its feet.

"Most countries have," said the Elegant Elephant shortly.

"He's got no right to order us around," said a Six, sitting up and jerking its thumb at Kabumpo.

"Yes—but!" Seven frowned at Six and put his hands over his ears. "This way," he said gruffly, and Kabumpo, stepping carefully, for many of the Figure Heads were still on their backs, followed Seven.

If the inhabitants of this strange city were queer, their city was even more so. The air was dry and choky and the houses were dull, oblong affairs, set in rows and rows with never a garden in sight. Each street had a large signpost on the corner, but they were not like the signs one usually sees in cities. For these were *plus* and *minus* signs with here and there a *long division* sign.

"I suppose everything in this street's divided up," mumbled Pompadore, looking up at a division sign curiously.

"Hope they don't subtract any of our belongings," whispered Kabumpo, as they turned into Minus Alley. "Look, Pompa, at the houses. Ever see anything like 'em before?"

"They remind me of something disagreeable," mused the Prince. "Why, they're *books*, Kabumpo, great big arithmetic books!" Pompa pointed at one.

"You mean they are shaped like books," said the Elegant Elephant. "I never saw books with windows and doors!"

"A lot you know!" said Seven, looking back scornfully, but Kabumpo was too interested to care. Out of the windows of the big book houses leaped hundreds of the little Figure Heads, and they laughed and jeered at Pompa and Kabumpo.

"Ho! Ho!" yelled one, leaning out so far it nearly fell on its Eight. "Wait till the Count sees 'em. He'll make an example of 'em!"

"What an awful country," whispered Pompadore, ducking just in time, as a Four snatched at his hair from an open window. But just then they turned a corner and entered a large gloomy court. Sitting on a square and solid wood throne, surrounded by a guard of Figure Heads, sat the Giant Ruler of this strange city.

"What have you got there, Seven?" roared the Ruler.

"I am the Elegant Elephant and this is the Prince of Pumperdink," announced Kabumpo before Seven could answer. Pompadore, himself, could say nothing for he had never before been addressed by a wooden Ruler in his life. And that is exactly what the King of the Figure Heads was—an ordinary school ruler, twice as large as a man, with arms and legs and a great square head set atop of his thin flat body.

"I don't care a rap *who* you are. I want to know *what* you are?" said the Ruler.

"We are travelers," spoke up Pompa, swallowing hard—"travelers in search of a Proper Princess."

"Well, you won't find any here," grunted the Ruler shortly. "We don't believe in 'em!"

"Would you mind telling me the name of your Kingdom," asked Pompa, somewhat cast down by these words.

"You have no heads," announced the Ruler calmly, "or you would have known that this is Rith Metic. *I*," he hammered himself upon the wooden chest—"I am its Ruler and every inch a King—King of the Figure Heads," he added, glaring around as if he expected someone to contradict him.

"All right! All right!" wheezed Kabumpo, bowing his head twice. "I knew twelve inches made a foot rule, but I never knew they made a King Rule. But could you give us some luncheon and allow us to pass peaceably through your Kingdom?"

"Pass through!" exclaimed the King, standing up indignantly. "We don't pass anyone through here. You've got to work your way through. Pass through, indeed! And when you've worked your way through we'll put you in a problem and make an example of you."

"They'll make a very good example, your Majesty," said a tall thin individual standing next to the Ruler. He eyed the two cunningly. "If a thin Prince sets out on a fat elephant to find a Proper Princess, how many yards of fringe will the elephant lose from his robe and how bald will the Prince be at the end of the journey? I don't believe anyone could figure that out," he murmured gleefully.

"It might be done by subtraction," said the King, looking at the two critically.

"Great hay stacks!" rumbled Kabumpo, glaring over his shoulder to see if he had lost any fringe so far. "What have we gotten into?"

"Bald!" gulped Pompa, rubbing his head. "Do you mean to say you take poor innocent travelers and make them into arithmetic problems?"

"Why not?" said the thin one, who looked exactly like a giant lead pencil. "And please address me as Count, after this—Count It Up is my name. What's the matter with living in a problem, my boy? Life is a problem, after all, and you will get used to it in time. I'll try to assign you to a comfortable book and you'll find book-keeping a lot more simple than house-keeping. This way, please!"

"Please go," yawned the Ruler, waving his hand. "The Count will take you in charge now." And so dazed was the Elegant Elephant by all this strange reasoning that he tamely followed the lead pencil person.

"Good-bye!" shouted the Ruler hoarsely. "Start them on simple additions," he said as they moved off.

The street ahead was filled with Figure Heads and as Kabumpo paused they began forming themselves into sums. The first row sat down, the next knelt behind them, the third stood up, the fourth nimbly leaped upon the shoulders of the third, and so on, until a long addition confronted the travelers.

"Now," said Count It Up in his blunt way, "as you haven't figures for heads, let us see if you have heads for figures." Kabumpo pushed back his pearl headdress and drops of perspiration began to run down his trunk. Prince Pompa, lying flat on Kabumpo's head, started to add up the first line of figures.

"Eighty-three," he announced anxiously.

"Say three and eight to carry," snapped Count It Up. "Here, Three!" A Three stepped out of the crowd and placed itself under the line. "I've got to be carried!" cried Eight, looking sulkily at Pompa.

"Carried!" snorted Kabumpo, snatching Eight into the air. "Well, I'll attend to you. You do the adding, Pompa, and I'll do the carrying."

He landed the Eight head down at the bottom of the line of Figure Heads and swung his trunk carelessly while he waited for his next victim. So, slowly and painfully, Pompa counted up the long lines and Kabumpo carried and if they made the slightest mistake the Figure Heads shouted with scorn and danced about till the confusion was terrible. When an example was finished, the Figure Heads in it marched away but another would immediately form lines ahead so that it took them a whole hour to go two blocks.

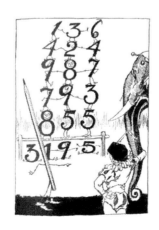

Slowly and Painfully Pompa Counted up the Long Lines

"Oh!" groaned Pompa at last, "We'll never get through this, Kabumpo. Look at those awful fractions ahead! Can't I skip fractions?" he asked looking pleadingly at Count It Up.

"Certainly not!" said the pencilly man stroking his shiny hair, which was straight and black and grew up into a sharp point. "You shall skip nothing!"

"That gives me an idea," whispered Kabumpo huskily. "Why shouldn't we skip altogether? We're bigger than they are. Why—"

"How are you getting on?" At the sound of that hoarse, familiar voice both the Prince and Kabumpo jumped.

"You don't mind me asking, I hope?" Clinging to the high picket fence and looking anxiously through the bars was the Curious Cottabus.

"Have you found the Greatest Common Divisor yet?"

"Who's he?" asked the Elegant Elephant suspiciously.

"Isn't there any way out of Rith Metic but this?" wailed Pompa, looking at the Cottabus pleadingly. He was too tired to mind being questioned.

The curious beast was delighted to have this new opportunity to talk to the travelers.

"Will you answer a few questions if I tell you?" asked the Cottabus, raising itself with great difficulty and looking over the palings.

"Yes—yes—anything," promised Pompa.

"Do you care for strawberry tarts?" asked the Cottabus, twitching its nose very rapidly.

"Of course," said the Prince. "Oh! Do hurry. Count It Up will be back in a moment!" He had run ahead to arrange a new problem and the rest of the Figure Heads paid no attention to the queer creature clinging to the palings.

"Are you going to invite the Scarecrow to your wedding?" gulped the Cottabus.

"I don't know any Scarecrow," said Pompa, "so how could I?"

"Are you fond of that old elephant?" The Cottabus waved at Kabumpo, who stamped first one foot then another and fairly snorted with rage.

"All right," sighed the Curious Cottabus, "that makes my fifty questions."

Hanging on to the fence with one paw it waved the other backward and forward as it chanted:

"How many tics in Rith Metic?
Tell me that and tell me quick!
But if you can't it's not my fault,
So simply turn a wintersault!"

The head of the Cottabus disappeared.

"Now isn't that provoking," gulped the Prince. "After it promised to help us, too!"

"I meant summersault," wheezed the Cottabus, reappearing suddenly—

"And if you can't it's not your fault,
So simply turn a summersault!"

it recited dolefully, and losing its balance fell off the fence and landed with a thud on the ground below.

"Here! Hurry along!" scolded Count It Up, prodding Kabumpo with a sharp pencil. "The next is a nice little problem in fractions."

"I wonder if it meant anything?" mused Pompadore, as Kabumpo approached the new problem. "'If you can't its not your fault, so simply turn a summersault.' Anyway it wouldn't hurt to try. Stop a minute, Kabumpo!"

Sliding down the Elegant Elephant's trunk, the Prince put his head on the ground and very carefully and deliberately turned a somersault. At his first motion Count It

Up gave a deafening scream, fell on his head and broke off his point, while the Figure Heads began to run in every direction.

"Do it again! Do it again!" cried Kabumpo joyfully. So Pompa turned another somersault and another, and another, and *another*, till not a Figure Head was in sight. Even the Figure Heads at the windows of the houses tumbled out and dashed madly around the corner. Before they could return, Kabumpo snatched up Pompa and tore through the deserted streets of Rith Metic till he came to the black iron gate at the other end of the city. Butting it open with his head, the Elegant Elephant dashed through and never stopped running till he was miles away from there.

"Have to rest a bit and eat some leaves," puffed Kabumpo, at last slowing down. "Whe—w!"

"Wish I could eat leaves," sighed the Prince, as Kabumpo began lunching off the tree tops. "But, never mind, we're out of Rith Metic! Wasn't it lucky that Cottabus followed us? I never would have thought of getting out of sums by somersaulting. Would you?"

"Only sensible thing it ever said, probably," answered the Elegant Elephant, with his mouth full of leaves. "There's a lot more to be learned by traveling than by studying, my boy. Somersaults for sums—let's always remember that!"

Pompa did not answer. He slid down Kabumpo's trunk and began hunting anxiously around for something to eat. Not far away he found a large nut tree and, gathering a handful of nuts, he sat down and began to crack them on a white marble slab near by. Next instant Kabumpo heard a thud and a muffled cry.

The Prince of Pumperdink had vanished, as if by magic.

"Where are you?" screamed the Elegant Elephant, pounding through the brush. "Pompa! Pompa! He's disappeared," gasped Kabumpo, rushing over to the marble slab. There was not a sign of the Royal Prince of Pumperdink anywhere, but carved carefully on the white stone were these words:

Please Knock Before You Fall In.

"Fall in!" snorted Kabumpo, his eyes rolling wildly. "Great Gooch!"

Chapter 6
Ruggedo's History In Six Rocks

On the same night that Prince Pompa and Kabumpo had disappeared from Pumperdink, a little gray gnome crouched in a deep chamber, tunneled under the Emerald City, laboriously carving letters on a big rock. It was Ruggedo, the old Gnome King, carving and grumbling and grumbling and carving, and pausing every few minutes to light his pipe with a hot coal which he kept in his pocket for that purpose. A big emerald lamp cast a green glow over the strange cavern and made the gnome look like a bad green goblin, which he was.

"Wag!" screamed the gnome, suddenly throwing down his chisel. "Where are you, you long-eared villain?" There was a slight stir at the back of the cave and a rabbit, of about the same size as the gnome, shuffled slowly forward.

"What you want?" he asked, rubbing one eye with his paw.

"Bring me a cup of melted mud, idiot!" roared the gnome, pounding on the rock. "And serve it to me on my throne at once!"

"Now, see here," the rabbit twitched his nose rapidly, "I'll get you a cup of melted mud, but don't you call me an idiot. I don't mind working for one, nor digging for one and listening to his foolishness, but nobody can call me an idiot—not even a make-believe King!"

"Oh, you make me tired!" fumed the gnome.

"Then go to sleep," advised the rabbit with a yawn. "What's the use of trying to pretend you're a King, Rug? Ho, ho! King over one wooden doll, six rocks and twenty-seven sofa cushions! You may have been a King once, but now you're just a plain gnome and nothing else, and if you go and sit quietly in your plain rocking chair I'll bring you a cup of plain mud."

With a chuckle, the rabbit retired, and Ruggedo, spluttering with fury, flounced into a doll's broken rocker that was set in the exact center of the cave.

"Here I give that rabbit everything I steal and he won't even allow me the little luxury of calling him an idiot or of pulling his ears. How can I pretend to be a King without an ear to pull?" grumbled the gnome.

"What are you grinning at?" Bouncing out of his chair, Ruggedo flew at a merry-faced wooden doll who sat propped up against the wall and shook her till her head turned round backwards and her arms and legs flew every which way. Then he hurled

24

her violently into a corner. Quite out of breath he sank back in his chair and stared angrily about.

When Wag returned the gnome snatched the tin cup of melted mud and tossed it down with one gulp. Then, flinging the cup at the doll, he went back to work.

The rabbit shook his head mournfully and, picking up the wooden doll, straightened her out and placed her on a cushion. Then, yawning again, he lit a candle and started for the passage at the back of the cave.

"How are you getting on?" he asked, pausing to look over the gnome's shoulder with a grin.

"Fine!" answered Ruggedo, forgetting to scowl. "I'm up to the sixth rock and expect to finish to-night."

"Who do you think will read it?" asked the rabbit, putting back both ears and stroking his whiskers. Then he gave a great spring, just escaped the chisel Ruggedo had flung at his head, and pattered away into the darkness. For several minutes the gnome danced up and down with fury. Then, as there was no one to pinch or shake, he started to work harder than ever on the sixth rock of his history. There were six of the great stones set in a row on one side of the cavern and the carving on them had taken the old gnome King the best part of two years. The letters were crooked and roughly chiseled, but quite readable. On the first rock he had carved:

History of Ruggedo in Six Rocks
Ruggedo the Rough—King of the Gnomes
One time Metal Monarch, at other times a Limoneag, a goose, a nut, and now a common gnome by order of
Ozma of Oz.

The second rock told of Ruggedo's magnificent Kingdom under the mountains of Ev, of the thousands of gnomes he had ruled and the great treasure of precious gems he had possessed, in those good old days before he was banished from his dominions.

The third rock told of his transformation of the Queen of Ev and her children into ornaments for his palace and of their rescue by a party from Oz, through the cleverness of Billina, a yellow hen. It told of the loss of his Magic Belt which was captured at this same time by Dorothy, a little girl from Kansas.

The fourth rock related how Ruggedo had tried to conquer Oz and recover his belt; how all of his plans failed and how he tumbled into the Fountain of Oblivion and forgot all about his campaign.

The fifth rock had taken Ruggedo the longest to carve, for it gave the story of his banishment by the Great Jinn Titihoochoo. You have probably read this story yourself. How Tik Tok, Betsy Bobbin, Shaggyman and Polychrome, trying to find Shaggy's brother, hidden in the Gnome King's metal forest, were thrown down a long tube to the other side of the world, and how the owner of the tube sent Quox, the dragon, to punish Ruggedo by banishment from his Kingdom and how Kaliko was made King of the Gnomes.

The sixth rock told of Ruggedo's last attempt to capture Oz. Meeting Kiki Aru, a Highup boy who knew a magic transformation word, Ruggedo suggested that they change themselves to Limoneags—queer beasts with lion heads, monkey tails and eagle wings—get all the beasts of Oz to help and march on the Emerald City. But this plan failed, too. Kiki lost his temper and changed Ruggedo to a goose, the Wizard of Oz discovered the magic word and changed both the conspirators to nuts. Later on they were changed back to their normal shapes, but again Ruggedo was plunged into the Fountain of Oblivion and again forgot his wicked plans. This ended the rock history, except for a short sentence stating that Ruggedo now lived in the Emerald City.

But the magic of the Fountain of Oblivion had soon worn off and it was not long before Ruggedo began to remember his past wickedness. That is why he decided to carve his life story in rock, so that it would be handy should he ever fall into the forgetful fountain again. And it had taken six rocks to tell all of his adventures. He had not carved these stories just as they had happened, nor ever called himself wicked, but he had told most of the facts, leaving out the parts most unflattering to himself. And now it was finished—his whole history in six rocks. Throwing down his chisel for the last time, Ruggedo straightened up and regarded his work with glowing pride.

"I don't believe there's another history like this in all Oz," puffed the gnome, tugging at his silver beard.

"It's a good thing," chuckled Wag, who had come back to eat a carrot. "Oz would not be a very happy place if there were many folks like you."

He seated himself quietly on the first rock of Ruggedo's history, and began nibbling his carrot.

"Get up! How dare you sit on my history?" Ruggedo stamped his foot and started threateningly toward Wag.

"All right," said the rabbit, "it's too hard, anyway."

"Of course it's hard," stormed Ruggedo. "I've had a hard life; hard as those rocks. Everybody's been against me from the very start, and all because I'm so little," he finished bitterly.

"No, because you are so wicked," said the rabbit calmly. "Now, don't throw your pipe at me, for you know it's the truth."

Ruggedo glared at the rabbit for a minute, then rushed over to the wooden doll, and began shaking her furiously. He always vented his rage on the wooden doll.

"Stop that," screamed Wag, "or I'll leave upon the spot. You ought to be ashamed of yourself. You old scrabble-scratch."

"She's not alive," snapped Ruggedo sulkily.

26

"How do you know?" retorted the rabbit. "Anyway, she's a jolly creature. I'm not going to have her banged around. Here you've taken her away from her little mother, and she hasn't even anyone to rock her to sleep."

"I'll rock her to sleep," screamed Ruggedo, maliciously. And flinging the doll on the floor he began hurling small rocks at the helpless little figure.

Scrambling to his feet, Wag rescued the wooden doll again, and Ruggedo, who really was afraid the rabbit would leave him, subsided into his rocking chair. Then reaching up to a small shelf over his head, he pulled down an accordion. At the first doleful wheeze Wag gave a great hop, dropped Peg and disappeared into his room in the farthest corner of the cave.

After his last attempt to capture Oz, the gnome had been given a small cottage to live in, just outside the Emerald City. But Ruggedo could not bear life above ground. The sunlight hurt his eyes, and the contented, happy faces of the people hurt his feelings, for he was exactly what Wag had called him—an old scrabble-scratch. So, while he pretended to live in the little cottage, according to Ozma's orders, he really spent most of his time in this deep, dark cave. He entered it by a secret passage, opening from his cellar.

Digging the long passage had been the hardest work Ruggedo had ever done in his bad little life. While toiling one day, he had bumped into the underground burrow of Wag, a wandering rabbit of Oz, and after a deal of bargaining, the rabbit had agreed to help him. Wag was to receive a ruby a month for his services, for the gnome still had a large bag of precious stones, which he had brought from the old Kingdom. After the bargain with Wag was made, the passage progressed rapidly, for the rabbit was an expert digger.

It was Ruggedo's idea to tunnel himself out a secret chamber, directly under Ozma's palace, and there establish a kingdom of his own. But when they had almost reached the spot, the earth began to crumble away, and a few strokes of Ruggedo's spade revealed a great dark cavern, already tunneled by someone else. It was huge and the exact shape of the royal palace. This Ruggedo discovered by careful measurement, and also that it was directly beneath the gorgeous green edifice, so that the footsteps of the servants could be heard faintly, pattering to and fro.

This dark, underground retreat suited the former Gnome King exactly and, without stopping to wonder to whom it had belonged, Ruggedo gleefully took possession. For almost two years he had lived here without anyone suspecting it, but so far his kingdom had not progressed very well. Wag had tried to coax some of his rabbit relations to serve the old gnome as subjects, but Ruggedo, besides his terrible temper, had a mean habit of pulling their ears, so that the whole crew had deserted the first week. He had pulled Wag's ears once, but the rabbit tore out a pawful of his whiskers, and bit him so severely in the leg that Ruggedo had never dared to try it again.

Wag had stayed partly because Ruggedo amused him and partly because of the bribes, for every day, in fear of losing his only retainer, Ruggedo brought Wag something from the Emerald City—something he had stolen! In return, Wag waited on the bad little gnome and listened to his grumblings against everybody in Oz. All the furnishings of this strange cave had been stolen from various houses in the Emerald City. The twenty-seven brocade cushions had been taken, one at a time from the palace; the green emerald lamp also. Every day Ruggedo ran innocently about the city, pretending to visit this one and that, and every day cups, spoons, and candlesticks disappeared.

The doll's rocker, which Ruggedo insisted upon calling his throne, had been taken from Betsy Bobbin, a little girl who lived with Ozma in the palace. He had lugged it through the secret passage with great difficulty. The wooden doll had been stolen from Trot, another of Ozma's companions. She was Trot's favorite doll, for she had been carved out of wood by Captain Bill, an old one-legged sailor, who was one of the most celebrated characters in all Oz. He had carved her for Trot one day when they were on a picnic in the Winkie Country, from the wood of a small yellow tree, and as Captain Bill had old-fashioned notions, Peg was a very old-fashioned doll. But she had splendid joints and could sit down and stand up. Her face was painted and as pleasant as laughing blue eyes, a turned-up nose, and a smiling mouth could make it. Trot had dressed her in a funny, old-fashioned dress, with pantalettes, and then, thinking Peg too short a name, the little girl had added Amy, because she was so amiable, she confided laughingly to the old sailor. Captain Bill had wagged his head understandingly, and Peg Amy had straightway become the most popular doll in the palace; that is, until she disappeared, for Ruggedo had found her one day in the garden and, chuckling wickedly, had carried her off to his cave.

How Trot would have felt if she had seen her poor doll being shaken and scolded by the old Gnome King! But Trot never knew. She hunted and hunted for her doll, and finally gave up in despair. Fortunately, Peg was well made, or she would have been shaken to bits, but her joints held bravely, and nothing—not even the terrible scolding of the bad old gnome—could change her pleasant expression.

Being the sole subject of so wicked a King, however, was wearing even for a wooden doll, and Peg was beginning to show signs of wear. Her nose was badly chipped, one pantalette was missing, and both sleeves had been jerked from her dress by the furious old gnome. If the rabbit was around, Ruggedo did not shake Peg as hard as he wanted to, but when the rabbit was gone, he pretended she was his old steward, Kaliko, and scolded and flung her about to his heart's content.

Ruggedo scolded and flung Peg about furiously

When not carving his history or shaking Peg, Ruggedo had spent most of his time digging new tunnels and chambers, so that leading off from the main cavern was a perfect network of underground passages. In the back of Ruggedo's head was a notion that some day he would conquer the Emerald City, regain his magic powers and then, after changing all the inhabitants to mouldy muffins, return to his dominions and oust Kaliko from his throne. Just how this was to be done, he had not decided, but the secret passages would be useful. So meanwhile he dug secret passages.

Above ground the little rascal went about so meekly and pretended to be so delighted with his life among the inhabitants of the Emerald City, that Ozma really thought he had reformed. Wag, to whom he confided his plans, would shake his head gloomily and often planned to leave the services of the wicked old gnome. There was no real harm in Wag, but the rabbit had a weakness for collecting, and the spoons, cups and odds and ends that Ruggedo brought him from the Emerald City filled him with delight. He felt that they were not gotten honestly, but his work for Ruggedo was honest and hard, "and it's not my fault if the old scrabble-scratch steals 'em," Wag would mumble to himself. In his heart he knew that he was doing wrong to stay with Ruggedo, but like all foolish creatures he could not make up his mind to go. So this very night, while the old gnome sat playing the accordion and howling doleful snatches of the Gnome National Air, Wag was gloating over his treasures. They quite filled his little dug-out room. There were two emerald plates, a gold pencil, a dozen china cups and saucers, twenty thimbles stolen from the work baskets of the good dames of Oz, scraps of silk, pictures and almost everything you could imagine.

"I'll soon have enough to marry and go to house-keeping on," murmured the rabbit, clasping his paws and twitching his nose very fast. He picked up a pair of purple wool socks that had once belonged to a little girl's doll and regarded them rapturously. Out of all the articles Ruggedo had given him, Wag considered these purple socks the most valuable, perhaps because they exactly fitted him and were the only things he could really use. The squeaking of the accordion stopped at last and, supposing his wicked little master had retired for the night, Wag prepared to enjoy himself. Draping a green silk scarf over his shoulders, he strutted before the mirror, pretending he was a Courtier of Oz. Then, throwing down the scarf, he sat down on the floor and had just drawn on one of the socks when a loud shrill scream from Ruggedo made his ears stand straight on end in amazement.

"What now?" coughed the rabbit, seizing the candle. Ruggedo was on his knees before the rocking chair.

"As I was sitting here, playing and singing," spluttered the old gnome, "I noticed a little ring in one of the rocks on the floor!"

"Well, what of it?" sniffed Wag, leaning down to pull up his sock.

"What of it?" shrieked the gnome. "What of it, you poor, puny earth worm! Look!" Leaning over Ruggedo's shoulder and dropping hot candle grease down the gnome's neck, Wag peered into a square opening in the floor. There lay a small gold box. Studded in gems on the lid were these words:

Glegg's Box of Mixed Magic.

"Mixed magic!" stuttered Wag, dropping the candle. "Oh, my socks and soup spoons!"

Ruggedo said nothing, but his little red eyes blazed maliciously. Reaching down, he lifted out the box and, clasping it to his fat little stomach, shook his fist at the high domed ceiling of the cave.

"Now!" hissed Ruggedo triumphantly. "Now we shall see what mixed magic will do to the Emerald City of Oz!"

30

Chapter 7
Sir Hokus And The Giants

"Oh!" sighed Sir Hokus of Pokes and Oz, stretching his armored legs to the fire. "How I yearn to slay a giant! How it would refresh me! Hast any real giants in Oz, Dorothy?"

"Don't you remember the candy giant?" laughed the little girl, looking up from the handkerchief she was making for Ozma.

"Not to my taste," said the Knight, "though his vest buttons were vastly nourishing."

"Well, there's Mr. Yoop—he's a real blood-and-bone giant. There are plenty of giants, I guess, if we knew just where to find them!" said the little girl, biting off her thread.

"Find 'em—bind 'em,

Get behind 'em!

Hokus Pokus

He don't mind 'em!"

screamed the Patch Work Girl, bounding out of her chair. "But why can't you stay peaceably at home, old Iron Sides, and be jolly like the rest of us?"

"You don't understand, Scraps," put in Dorothy gravely. "Sir Hokus is a Knight and it is a true Knight's duty to slay giants and dragons and go on quests!"

"*That* it is, my Lady Patches!" boomed Sir Hokus, puffing out his chest. "I've rusted here in idleness long enough. To-morrow, with Ozma's permission, I shall start on a giant quest."

"I'd go with you, only I've promised to help Ozma count the royal emeralds," said the Scarecrow, who had ridden over from his Corn-Ear residence to spend a week with his old friends in the Emerald City.

"Giants, Sir, are bluff and rude

And might mistake a man for food!

Hokus Pokus, be discreet,

31

Or you will soon be giant meat!"
chuckled the Patch Work Girl, crooking her finger under the Knight's nose.

"Nonsense!" blustered Sir Hokus, waving Scraps aside. Rising from his green arm chair, he strode up and down the room, his armor clanking at every step. Straightway the company began to tell about wild giants they had read of or known. Trot and Betsy Bobbin held hands as they sat together on the sofa, and Toto, Dorothy's small dog, crept closer to his little mistress, the bristles on his back rising higher as each story was finished. "Giant stories are all very well, but why tell 'em at night?" shivered Toto, peering nervously at the long shadows in the corners of the room.

It was the evening after Ruggedo's strange discovery of the mixed magic and in the royal palace Ozma and most of the Courtiers had retired. But a few of Princess Dorothy's special friends had gathered in the cozy sitting-room of her apartment to talk about old times. They were very unusual and interesting friends, not at all the sort one would expect to find in a royal palace, even in Fairyland. Dorothy, herself, before she had become a Princess of Oz, had been a little girl from Kansas but, after several visits to this delightful country, she had preferred to make Oz her home.

Trot and Betsy Bobbin also had come from the United States by way of shipwrecks, so to speak, and had been invited to remain by Ozma, the little fairy Princess who ruled Oz, and now each of these girls had a cozy little apartment in the royal palace. Toto had come with Dorothy, but the rest of the company were of more or less magic extraction.

The Scarecrow, a stuffed straw person, with a marvelous set of mixed brains given to him by the Wizard of Oz, was Dorothy's favorite. In fact she had discovered him herself upon a Munchkin farm, lifted him down from his bean pole and brought him to the Emerald City. Tik Tok was a wonderful man made entirely of copper, who could talk, think and act as well as the next fellow when properly wound. You would have been amazed to hear the giant story he was ticking off at this very minute. As for Scraps, she had been made by a magician's wife out of old pieces of patch-work and magically brought to life. Her bright patches, yarn hair and silver suspender button eyes gave Scraps so comical an expression that just to look at her tickled one's funny bone. Her head was full of nonsense rhymes and she was so amusing and cheerful that Ozma insisted upon her living with the rest of the celebrities in the Emerald City.

32

Just to Look at Scraps Tickled One's Funny Bone

Sir Hokus of Pokes was a comparative new-comer in the capital city of Oz. Yet the Knight was so old that it would give me lumbago just to try to count up his birthdays. He dated back to King Arthur, in fact, and had been wished into the Land of Oz centuries before by an enemy sorcerer. Dorothy had found and rescued him, with the Cowardly Lion's help, from Pokes, the dullest Kingdom in Oz. As there were no other Knights in the Emerald City, Sir Hokus was much stared at and admired. Even the Soldier with the Green Whiskers, the one and only soldier and entire army of Oz—yes, even the soldier with the Green Whiskers saluted Sir Hokus when he passed. Ozma, herself, felt more secure since the Knight had come to live in the palace. He was well versed in adventure and always courageous and courteous, withal.

But, while I've been telling you all this, Tik Tok had finished his story of a three-legged giant who lived in Ev.

"And where is Ev?" puffed Sir Hokus, planting himself before Tik Tok.

"Ev," began Tik Tok in his precise fashion, "is to the north-west of here on the other side of the im—" There was a whirr and a click and the copper man stood motionless and soundless, his round eyes fixed solemnly on the Knight.

"Pass-able des-ert," finished the Scarecrow, jumping up and kindly winding all of Tik Tok's keys as if nothing had happened.

"Pass-able des-ert," continued the Copper Man.

"That's where the old Gnome King used to live," piped Betsy Bobbin, bouncing up and down upon the sofa, "under the mountains of Ev, and he threw us down a tube and tried to melt you in a crucible, didn't he, Tik Tok?"

"He was a ve-ry bad per-son," said the Copper Man.

"Ruggedo was a wicked King,
'Tho' now he's good as pie,
But none the less, I must confess,
He has a wicked eye!"

burst out Scraps, who was tired of sitting still listening to giant stories.

But Sir Hokus could not be got off the subject of giants. "To Ev!" thundered the Knight, raising his sword. "To-morrow I'm off to Ev to conquer this terrible monster. Large as a mountain, you say, Tik Tok? Well, what care I for mountains? I, Sir Hokus of Pokes, will slay him!"

"Hurrah for the giant killer!" giggled Scraps, turning a somersault and nearly falling in the fire.

"Let's go to bed!" said Dorothy uneasily. She had for the last few minutes been hearing strange rumbles. Of course it could not be giants; still the conversation, she concluded, had better be finished by sunlight.

But it never was, for at that moment there was a deafening crash. The lights went out; the whole castle shivered; furniture fell every which way. Down clattered Sir Hokus, falling with a terrible clangor on top of the Copper Man. Down rolled the little girls and the Scarecrow and Scraps. Down tumbled everybody.

"Cyclone!" gasped Dorothy, who had experienced several in Kansas.

"Giants!" stuttered Betsy Bobbin, clutching Trot.

The Wizard of Oz tried to reassure the agitated company. He told them there was no cause for alarm, and that they would soon find out what was the trouble. The soothing words of the Wizard were scarcely heard.

The Smiling Little Wizard of Oz

What the others said was lost in the noise that followed. Thumps—bangs—crashes—screams came from every room in the rocking palace.

"We're flying! The whole castle's flying up in the air!" screamed Dorothy. Then she subsided, as an emerald clock and three pictures came thumping down on her head.

What had happened? No one could say. Dorothy, Betsy Bobbin and Trot had fainted dead away. The Scarecrow and Sir Hokus were tangled up on the floor, clasped in each other's arms.

The confusion was terrific. Only the Wizard was still calm and smiling.

Chapter 8
Woe In The Emerald City

The Soldier with the Green Whiskers finished his breakfast slowly, combed his beard, pinned on all of his medals and solemnly issued forth from his little house at the garden gates.

"Forward march!" snapped the soldier. He had to give himself orders, being the only man, general or private in the army. And forward march he did. It was his custom to report to Ozma every morning to receive his orders for the day. When he had gone through the little patch of trees that separated his cottage from the palace, the Soldier with the Green Whiskers gave a great leap.

"Halt! Break ranks!" roared the Grand Army of Oz, clutching his beard in terror. "Great Goloshes!" He rubbed his eyes and looked again. Yes, the gorgeous emerald-studded palace had disappeared, leaving not so much as a gold brick to tell where it had stood. Trembling in every knee, the Grand Army of Oz approached. A great black hole, the exact shape of the palace, yawned at his feet. He took one look down that awful cavity, then shot through the palace gardens like a green comet.

Like Paul Revere he had gone to give the alarm, and Paul Revere himself never made better time. He thumped on windows and banged on doors and dashed through the sleeping city like a whirlwind. In five minutes there was not a man, woman or child who did not know of the terrible calamity. They rushed to the palace gardens in a panic. Some stared up in the air; others peered down the dark hole; still others ran about wildly trying to discover some trace of the missing castle.

"What shall we do?" they wailed dismally. For to have their lovely little Queen and the Wizard and all the most important people in Oz disappear at once was simply terrifying. They were a gentle and kindly folk, used to obeying orders, and now there was no one to tell them what to do.

At last Unk Nunkie, an old Munchkin who had taken up residence in the Emerald City, pushed through the crowd. Unk was a man of few words, but a wise old chap for all that, so they made way for him respectfully. First Unk Nunkie stroked his beard; then pointing with his long lean finger toward the south he snapped out one word—"GLINDA!"

Of course! They must tell Glinda. Why had they not thought of it themselves? Glinda would know just what to do and how to do it. Three cheers for Unk Nunkie! Glinda, you know, is the good Sorceress of Oz, who knows more magic than anyone in the Kingdom, but who only practices it for the people's good. Indeed, Glinda and the Wizard of Oz are the only ones permitted to practice magic, for so much harm had come of it that Ozma made a law forbidding sorcery in all of its branches. But even in a fairy country people do not always obey the laws and everyone felt that magic was at the bottom of this disaster.

So away to fetch Glinda dashed the Grand Army, his green whiskers streaming behind him. Fortunately the royal stables had not disappeared with the palace, so the gallant army sprang upon the back of the Saw Horse, and without stopping to explain to the other royal beasts, bade it carry him to Glinda as fast as it could gallop. Being made of wood with gold shod feet and magically brought to life, the Saw Horse can run faster than any animal in Oz. It never tired or needed food and when it understood that the palace and its dear little Mistress had disappeared it fairly flew; for the Saw Horse loved Ozma with all its saw dust and was devoted as only a wooden beast can be.

The Grand Army sprang upon the back of the Saw Horse

In an hour they had reached Glinda's shining marble palace in the southern part of the Quadling country, and as soon as the lovely Sorceress had heard the soldier's story, she hurried to the magic Book of Records. This is the most valuable book in Oz and it is kept padlocked with many golden chains to a gold table, for in this great volume appear all the events happening in and out of the world.

Now, Glinda had been so occupied trying to discover the cause of frowns that she had not referred to the book for several days and naturally there were many pages to go over. There were hundreds of entries concerning automobile accidents in the United States and elsewhere. These Glinda passed over hurriedly, till she came to three sentences printed in red, for Oz news always appeared in the book in red letters. The first sentence did not seem important. It merely stated that the Prince of Pumperdink was journeying toward the Emerald City. The other two entries seemed serious.

"Glegg's box of Mixed Magic has been discovered," said the second, and "Ruggedo has something on his *mind*," stated the third. Glinda pored over the book for a long time to see whether any more information would be given but not another red sentence appeared. With a sigh, Glinda turned to the Soldier with the Green Whiskers.

"Ruggedo Has Something on His Mind," Read Glinda

"The old Gnome King must be mixed up in this," she said anxiously, "and as he was last seen in the Emerald City, I will return with you at once." So Glinda and the Soldier with the Green Whiskers flew back to the Emerald City drawn in Glinda's chariot by swift flying swans and the little Saw Horse trotted back by himself. When they reached the gardens a great crowd had gathered by the Fountain of Oblivion and a tall green grocer was speaking excitedly.

"What is it?" asked Glinda, shuddering as she passed the dreadful hole where Ozma's lovely palace had once stood. Everyone started explaining at once so that Glinda was obliged to clap her hands for silence.

"Foot print!" Unk Nunkie stood upon his tip toes and whispered it in Glinda's ear and when she looked where Unk pointed she saw a huge, shallow cave-in that crushed the flower beds for as far as she could see.

"Foot print!" gasped Glinda in amazement.

"Uh huh!" Unk Nunkie wagged his head determinedly and then, pulling his hat down over his eyes, spoke his last word on the subject: "*GIANT!*"

"A giant foot print! Why so it is!" cried Glinda.

"What shall we do? What shall we do?" cried the frightened inhabitants of the Emerald City, wringing their hands.

"First, find Ruggedo," ordered Glinda, suddenly remembering the mysterious entry in the Book of Records. So, away to the little cottage hurried the crowd. They searched it from cellar to garret, but of course found no trace of the wicked little gnome. As no one knew about the secret passage in Ruggedo's cellar, they never thought of searching underground.

Meanwhile Glinda sank down on one of the golden garden benches and tried to think. The Comfortable Camel stumbled broken-heartedly across the lawn and dropping on its knees begged the Sorceress in a tearful voice to save Sir Hokus of Pokes. The Camel and the Doubtful Dromedary had been discovered by the Knight on his last adventure and were deeply attached to him. Soon all the palace pets came and stood in a dejected row before Glinda—Betsy's mule, Hank, hee-hawing dismally and the Hungry Tiger threatening to eat everyone in sight if any harm came to the three little girls.

"I doubt if we'll ever see them again," groaned the Doubtful Dromedary, leaning up against a tree.

"Oh Doubty—how *can* you?" wailed the Camel, tears streaming down its nose.

"Please do be quiet," begged Glinda, "or I'll forget all the magic I know. Let me see, now—how does one catch a marauding giant who has run off with a castle?"

On her fingers Glinda counted up all the giants in the four countries of Oz. No! It could not be an Oz giant; there was none large enough. It must be a giant from some strange country.

When the crowd returned with the news that Ruggedo had disappeared Glinda felt more uneasy still. But hiding her anxiety she bade the people return to their homes and continue their work and play as usual. Then, promising to return that evening with a plan to save the castle, and charging the Soldier with the Green Whiskers to keep a strict watch in the garden, Glinda stepped into her chariot and flew back to the South. All that day, in her palace in the Quadling country, Glinda bent over her encyclopedia on giants, and far into the night the lights burned from her high turret-chamber, as she consulted book after book of magic.

Chapter 9
Mixed Magic Makes Mischief

The Book of Records had been perfectly correct in stating that Ruggedo had something on his mind. *He had!* To understand the mysterious disappearance of Ozma's palace, we must go back to the old Ex-King of the Gnomes. The whole of the night after he had found Glegg's box of Mixed Magic, Ruggedo had spent trying to open the box. But pry and poke as he would it stubbornly refused to give up its secrets.

"Better come to bed," advised Wag, twitching his nose nervously. "Mixed Magic isn't safe, you know. It might explode."

"Idiot!" grumbled Ruggedo. "I don't know who Glegg is or was, but I'm going to find out what kind of magic he mixes. I'm going to open this box if it takes me a century."

"All right," quavered Wag, retiring backward and holding up his paw. "All right, but remember I warned you! Don't meddle with magic, that's my motto!"

"I don't care a harebell what your motto is," sneered the gnome, continuing to hammer on the gold lid.

When he reached his room, Wag shut the door and sank dejectedly upon the edge of the bed.

"There's no manner of use trying to stop him," sighed the rabbit, "so I've got to get out of here before he gets me into trouble. I'll go to-morrow!" resolved Wag, pulling his long ear nervously. With this good resolution, the little rabbit drooped off asleep.

Very cautiously he opened the door of his little rock-room next morning. Ruggedo was sound asleep on the floor, his head on the magic box, and Peg Amy, with her wooden arms and legs flung out in every direction, lay sprawled in a corner.

Been shaking you again, the old scrabble-scratch!" whispered the rabbit indignantly, "just 'cause he couldn't open that box. Well, never mind, Peg, I'm leaving to-day and as surely as I've ears and whiskers you shall go too!" Picking up the poor wooden doll Wag tucked her under his arm. Was it imagination, or did the little wooden face break into a sunny smile? It seemed so to Wag and, with a real thrill of pleasure, he tip-toed back to his room and began tossing his treasures into one of the bed sheets. He seated Peg in his own small rocking chair and from time to time he nodded to her reassuringly.

"We'll soon be out now, my dear," he chuckled, quite as if Peg had been alive. She often did seem alive to Wag. "Then we'll see what Ozma has to say to this Mixed Magic," continued the bunny, wiggling his ears indignantly. And so occupied was he collecting his treasures that he did not hear Ruggedo's call and next minute the angry gnome himself stood in the doorway.

"What does this mean?" he cried furiously, pointing to the tied up sheet. Then he stamped his foot so hard that Peg Amy fell over sideways in the chair and all the ornaments in the room skipped as if alive.

The rabbit whirled 'round in a hurry.

"It means I'm leaving you for good, you wicked little monster!" shrilled Wag, his whiskers trembling with agitation and his ears sticking straight out behind. "*Leaving*—do you hear?"

Then he snatched Peg Amy in one paw and his treasures in the other and tried to brush past Ruggedo. But the gnome was too quick for him. Springing out of the room, he slammed the door and locked it. Wag could hear him rolling up rocks for further security.

"Thought you'd steal a march on old Ruggedo; thought you'd tell Ozma all his plans and get a nice little reward! Well, *think again!*" shouted the gnome through the keyhole.

Wag had plenty of time to think, for Ruggedo never came near the rabbit's room all day. At every sound poor Wag leaped into the air, for he felt sure each blow could only mean the opening of the dreaded magic box. To reassure himself he held long conversations with the wooden doll and Peg's calm cheerfulness steadied him a lot.

"I might dig my way out but it would take so long! My ear tips! How provoking it is!" exclaimed Wag. "But perhaps he'll relent by nightfall!" Slowly the day dragged on but nothing came from the big rock room but thumps, grumbles and bangs.

"It is fortunate that you do not eat, Peg, dear," sighed the rabbit late in the afternoon, nibbling disconsolately on a stale biscuit he had found under his bureau. "Shall you care very much if I starve? I probably shall, you know. Of course no one in Oz can die, but starving forever is not comfortable either." At this the wooden doll seemed to shake her head, as much as to say: "You won't starve, Wag dear; just be patient a little longer." Not that she really said this, mind you, but Wag knew from her smile that this is what she was thinking.

It was hot and stuffy in the little rock chamber and the faint light that filtered down from the hole in the ceiling was far from cheerful. At last night came, and that was worse. Wag lit his only candle but it was already partly burned down and soon with a dismal sputter it went out and left the two sitting in the dark. Peg Amy stared cheerfully ahead but the rabbit, worn out by his long day of fright and worry, fell into a heavy slumber.

Meanwhile Ruggedo had worked on the magic box and every minute he became more impatient. All his poundings failed to make even a dent on the gold lid and even jumping on it brought no result. The little gnome had eaten nothing since morning and by nightfall he was stamping around the box in a perfect fury. His eyes snapped and twinkled like live coals and his wispy white hair fairly crackled with rage. Hidden in this box were magic secrets that would doubtless enable him to capture the Whole of Oz but, *klumping kaloogas*, how was he to get at 'em? He finally gave the gold box such a vindictive kick that he almost crushed his curly toes; then holding onto one foot, he hopped about on the other till he fell over exhausted.

For several minutes he lay perfectly still; then jumping up he seized the box and flung it with all his gnome might against the rock wall.

"Take that!" screamed Ruggedo furiously. There was a bright flash; then the box righted itself slowly and sailed straight back into Ruggedo's hands and, more wonderful still, *it was open*! With his eyes almost popping from his head, the gnome sat down on the floor, the box in his lap.

40

In the first tray were four golden flasks and each one was carefully labeled. The first was marked, "Flying Fluid"; "Vanishing Cream" was in the second. The third flask held "Glegg's Instantaneous Expanding Extract," and in the fourth was "Spike's Hair Strengthener."

Ruggedo rubbed his hands gleefully and lifted out the top tray. In the next compartment was a tiny copper kettle, a lamp and a package marked "Triple Trick Tea." So anxious was Ruggedo to know what was in the last compartment that he scarcely glanced at Glegg's tea set. Quickly he peered into the bottom of the casket. There were two boxes. Taking up the first Ruggedo read, "Glegg's Question Box. Shake three times after each question."

"Great Grampus!" spluttered the gnome, "this is a find!" He was growing more excited every minute and his hands shook so he could hardly read the label on the last box. Finally he made it out: "Re-animating Rays, guaranteed to reawaken any person who has lost the power of life through sorcery, witchcraft or enchantment," said the label.

Well, did anyone ever hear anything more magic than that? Ruggedo glanced from one to the other of the little gold flasks and boxes. There were so many he hardly knew which to use first. "Flying Fluid and Vanishing Cream," mused the gnome. Well, they might help after he had captured Oz, but he felt it would take more powerful magic than Flying Fluid and Vanishing Cream to capture the fairy Kingdom. Next he picked up the bottle labeled "Spike's Hair Strengthener." Anything that strengthened would be helpful, so, with one eye on the last bottle, Ruggedo absently rubbed some of the hair strengthener on his head. He stopped rubbing in a hurry and put his finger in his mouth with a howl of pain. Then he jumped up in alarm and ran to a small mirror hanging on the wall. Every hair on his head had become an iron spike and the result was so terrible that it frightened even the old gnome. He flung the bottle angrily on the ground. But stop! He could butt his enemies with the sharp spikes! Comforting himself with this cheerful thought, Ruggedo returned to the magic box.

"Instantaneous Expanding Extract," muttered the gnome, turning the bottle over carefully. "That ought to make me *larger*—and if I were larger—if I were larger!" He snapped his fingers and began hopping up and down. He was about to empty the bottle over his head when he suddenly reflected that it might be safer to try this powerful extract on someone else. But on whom?

Ruggedo glanced quickly around the cave and then remembered the wooden doll. He would try a little on Peg Amy and see how it worked. Turning the key he stepped softly into Wag's room. Without wakening the rabbit, Ruggedo dragged out the wooden doll. Propping her up against the wall, the gnome uncorked the bottle of expanding fluid and dropped two drops on Peg Amy's head. Peg was about ten inches high, but no sooner had the expanding fluid touched her than she shot up four feet and with such force that she lost her balance and came crashing down on top of Ruggedo, almost crushing him flat.

"Get off, you great log of wood!" screamed the gnome, struggling furiously. But this Peg Amy was powerless to do and it was only after a frightful struggle that Ruggedo managed to drag himself out. He started to shake Peg but as she was now four times his size he soon gave that up.

 "Well, anyway it works," sighed the gnome, rubbing his nose and the middle of his back. "I wonder how it would act on a live person? I'll try a little on that silly rabbit," he concluded, tip-toeing back into Wag's room. Now Wag's apartment was about seven feet square—plenty large enough for a regular rabbit—but two drops of the expanding fluid—and, *stars*! Wag was no longer a regular rabbit but a six-foot funny bunny, stretching from one end of the room to the other. He expanded without even waking up. Ruggedo had to squeeze past him in order to get out and, chuckling with satisfaction, the gnome hurried back to his box of magic. His mind was now made up. He would take Glegg's Mixed Magic under his arm, go above ground and with the Expanding Fluid change himself into a giant. Then conquering Oz would be a simple matter.

It was all going to be so easy and amusing that Ruggedo felt he had plenty of time to examine the rest of the bottles and boxes. He rubbed some of the Vanishing Cream on a sofa cushion and it instantly disappeared. The box of Re-animating Rays, guaranteed to reawaken anyone from enchantment, interested the old gnome immensely, but how could he try them when there was no bewitched person about— at least none that he knew of? Then his eye fell on the Question Box. Why not try that? So, "How shall I use the Re-animating Rays?" asked Ruggedo, shaking the box three times. Nothing happened at first. Then, by the light from his emerald lamp, the gnome saw a sentence forming on the lid.

"Try them on Peg," said the box shortly. Without thinking of consequences or wondering what the Question Box meant by suggesting Peg, the curious gnome opened the box of rays and held it over the huge wooden doll. For as long as it would take to count ten Peg lay perfectly still. Then, with a creak and jerk, she sprang to her feet.

"How perfectly pomiferous!" cried Peg Amy, with an awkward jump. "I'm alive! Why, I'm alive all over!" She moved one arm, then the other and turned her head stiffly from side to side. "I can walk!" cried Peg. "I can walk; I can skip; I can run!" Here Peg began running around the cave, her joints squeaking merrily at every step.

At Peg's first move Ruggedo had jumped back of a rock, his every spike standing on end. Too late he realized his mistake. This huge wooden creature clattering around the cave was positively dangerous. Why, she might easily pound him to bits. Why on earth had he meddled with the magic rays and why under the earth should a wooden doll come to life? He waited till Peg had run to the farthest end of the cave; then he dashed to the magic casket and scrambled the bottles, the Trick Tea Set and the flasks back into place and started for the door that led to the secret passage as fast as his crooked little legs would carry him.

But he was not fast enough, for Peg heard and like a flash was after him.

"Stop! Go away!" screamed Ruggedo.

"Why, it's the old gnome!" cried the Wooden Doll in surprise. "The wicked old gnome who used to shake me all the time. Why, how small he is! I could pick him up with one hand!" She made a snatch at Ruggedo.

"Go away!" shrieked Ruggedo, ducking behind a rock. "Go away—there's a dear girl," he added coaxingly. "I didn't shake you much—not too much, you know!"

Peg Amy put a wooden finger to her forehead and regarded him attentively.

"I remember," she murmured thoughtfully. "You found a magic box, and you're going to harm Ozma and try to conquer Oz. I must get that box!"

Reaching around the rock she seized Ruggedo by the arm.

In a panic, he jerked away. "Help! Help!" cried the gnome King, darting off toward the other end of the cave. "Help! Help!"

In his little rock room Wag stirred uneasily. Then, as Ruggedo's cries grew louder, he bounced erect and almost cracked his skull on the low ceiling. Hardly knowing what he was doing he rushed at the door only to knock himself almost senseless against the top, for of course he did not realize he had expanded into a giant rabbit. But as the cries from the other room became louder and louder he got up and rubbing his head in a dazed fashion he somehow crowded himself through the door and hopped into the cave. When he saw Peg Amy chasing Ruggedo, Wag fell back against the wall.

"My wocks and hoop soons!" stuttered the rabbit. "She is alive! And he's shrunk!"

Wag's voice rose triumphantly. "I'm going to pound his curly toes off!" he shouted. With this he joined merrily in the chase.

"I'll catch him!" he called, "I'll catch him, Peg, my dear, and make him pay for all the shakings he has given you. I'll pound his curly toes off!"

"Oh, Wag! Don't do that," cried the Wooden Doll, stopping short. "I didn't mind the shakings and gnomes don't know any better!"

"Neither do rabbits!" cried Wag stubbornly, bounding after Ruggedo. "I'll pound his curly toes off, I tell you!"

The old gnome was sputtering like a firecracker. What chance had he now with two after him? Then suddenly he had an idea. Without stopping, he fumbled in the box

43

which he still clutched under one arm and pulled out the bottle of Expanding Fluid. Uncorking the bottle he poured its contents over his head—*every single drop!*

This is what happened: First he shot out sideways, till Peg and Wag were almost crushed against the wall. With a hoarse scream Wag dragged Peg Amy back into his room, which was now barely large enough to hold them. They were just in time, for Ruggedo was still spreading. Soon there was not an inch of space left to expand in. Then he shot up and grew up and grew and grew and groaned and grew till there wasn't any more room to grow in. So, he burst through the top of the cave, with a noise like fifty boilers exploding.

No wonder Dorothy thought it was a cyclone! For what was on the top of the cave but the royal palace of Oz? The next instant it was impaled fast on the spikes of Ruggedo's giant head and shooting up with him toward the clouds. And that wretched gnome never stopped growing till he was three-quarters of a mile high!

The royal palace of Oz impaled fast on the spikes of Ruggedo's giant head

If the people in the palace were frightened, Ruggedo was more frightened still. Being a giant was a new experience for him and having a castle jammed on his head was worse still. The first thing he tried to do, when he stopped growing, was to lift the castle off, but his spikes were driven fast into the foundations and it fitted closer than his scalp.

In a panic Ruggedo began to run, and when a giant runs he gets somewhere. Each step carried him a half mile and shook the country below like an earthquake and rattled the people in the castle above like pennies in a Christmas bank. Shaking with terror and hardly knowing why, the gnome made for his old Kingdom, and in an hour had reached the little country of Oogaboo, which is in the very northwestern corner of OZ, opposite his old dominions.

The Deadly Desert is so narrow at this point that with one jump Ruggedo was across and, puffing like a volcano about to erupt, he sank down on the highest mountain in Ev. Fortunately he had not stepped on any cities in his flight, although he had crushed several forests and about a hundred fences.

"Oh, Oh, My head!" groaned Ruggedo, rocking to and fro. He seemed to have forgotten all about conquering Oz. He was full of twinges and growing pains.

Ozma's castle was giving him a thundering headache, and there he sat, a fearsome figure in the bright moonlight, moaning and groaning instead of conquering.

The Book of Records had been right indeed when it stated that Ruggedo had something on his mind. Ozma's castle itself sat squarely upon that mischievous mind—and every moment it seemed to grow heavier.

No wonder there had been confusion in the castle! Every time Ruggedo shook his aching head Ozma and her guests were tossed about like leaves in a storm. Mixed magic had made mischief indeed.

Chapter 10
Peg and Wag To The Rescue

For a long time after the terrific bang following Ruggedo's final expansion, Wag and Peg Amy had been too stunned to even move. Crowded together in the little rock room, they lay perfectly breathless.

"Umpthing sappened," quavered the rabbit at last.

"That sounds rather queer, but I think I know what you mean," said Peg, sitting up cautiously.

"Something has happened. Ruggedo's been blown up, I guess."

"Mixed Magic!" groaned Wag gloomily. "I knew it would explode. Say, Peg, what makes this room so small?"

"I don't know," sighed the doll in a puzzled voice, for neither Peg nor Wag realized how much they had grown. "But let's go above ground and see what has become of Ruggedo." One at a time and with great difficulty they got through the door.

"Why, there are the stars!" cried Peg Amy, clasping her wooden hands rapturously. "Real stars!" The top of the cave had gone off with the old gnome King and the two stood looking up at the lovely skies of Oz.

"It doesn't seem so high as it used to," said the rabbit, looking at the walls. "Why, I believe I could jump out if I took a good run and carry you, too. Come ashort, Peg!"

"Aren't you mixed, Wag dear? Don't you mean come along?" asked Peg, smoothing down her torn dress.

"Well, now that you mention it, my head does feel queer," admitted the rabbit, twitching his nose, "bort of sackwards!"

"Sort of backwards," corrected Peg gently. "Well, never mind. I know what you mean. But do let's try to find that awful box of magic. You know Ruggedo brought me to life, Wag, with something in that box!"

"Only good thing he ever did," said Wag, shaking his head. "But I think you were alive before," he added solemnly. "You always seemed alive to me."

"I think so, too," whispered Peg excitedly. "I can't remember just how, or where, but Oh! Wag! I know I've been alive before. I remember dancing."

Peg took a few awkward steps and Wag looked on dubiously, too polite to criticize her efforts. He didn't even laugh when Peg Amy fell down. Peg laughed herself, however, as merrily as possible. "It's going to be such fun being alive," she said, picking herself up gaily, "such fun, Wag dear. Why, there's Glegg's box!" She pounced upon the little shining gold casket. "Ruggedo didn't take it after all!"

"Is it shut?" asked Wag, clapping both paws to his ears. "Look out for explosions, say I."

"No, but I'll soon close it," said Peg and, shutting Glegg's box, she slipped it into pocket of her dress. It was about half the size of this book you are reading and as Peg's pockets were big and old fashioned, it fitted quite nicely.

"Come ashort," said Wag again, looking around uneasily, for he was anxious to get out of the gnome's cave. So Peg seated herself carefully on his back and clasped her wooden arms around his neck. Then Wag ran back a few steps, gave a great jump and sailed up, up and out of the cave.

"Ten penny tea cups!" shrieked the Soldier with the Green Whiskers, falling over backwards. "What next?" For Wag with Peg on his back had leaped straight over his head.

Picking himself up, and with every whisker in his beard prickling straight on end, the Grand Army of Oz backed toward the royal stable. When he had backed half the distance he turned and ran for his life. But he need not have been afraid.

"What a funny little man," chuckled Wag. "Why, he's no bigger than we are. He's no—!" Then suddenly Wag clutched his ears. "Oh!" he screamed, beginning to hop up and down, "I forgot all my treasures—my olden goop soons. Oh! Oh! My urple sool wocks! I've forgotten my urple sool wocks!"

"Your what?" cried Peg Amy, clutching him by the fur. "Now Wag, dear, you're all mixed up. Perhaps it's 'cause your ears are crossed. There, now, do stop wiggling your whiskers and turn out your toes!"

But Wag continued to wiggle his whiskers and turn in his toes and roar for his urple sool wocks.

"Stop!" screamed Peg at last, with both hands over her wooden ears. "I know what you mean! Your purple wool socks!"

"Yes," sobbed the rabbit, slumping down on a rock and holding his head in both paws.

"Well, don't you think"—the Wooden Doll shook her head jerkily—"Don't you think it's just as well? Ruggedo stole all those things and you wouldn't want stolen soup spoons, now would you?"

Wag took a long breath and regarded Peg uncertainly. Then something in her pleasant wooden face seemed to brace him up.

"No!" he sighed solemnly—"I s'pose not. I ought to have left Rug long ago."

"But then you couldn't have helped me," said Peg brightly. "Let's don't think about it any more. You've been awfully good to me, Wag."

"Have I?" said Wag more cheerfully. "Well, you're a good sort, Peg—a regular Princess!" he finished, puffing out his chest, "and anything you say goes."

"Princess?" laughed the Wooden Doll, pleased nevertheless. "I'm a funny Princess, in this old dress. Did you ever hear of a wooden Princess, Wag?"

"You look like a Princess to me," said the rabbit stoutly. "Dresses don't matter."

This speech so tickled the Wooden Doll that she gave Wag a good hug and began dancing again. "Being alive is such fun!" she called gaily over her shoulder, "and you are so wonderful!"

Wag's chest expanded at least three inches and his whiskers trembled with emotion. "Hop on my back Peg and I'll take you anywhere you want to go," he puffed magnificently.

But the Wooden Doll had suddenly grown sober. "Wherever is the castle?" she cried anxiously. She remembered exactly where it had stood when she was an unalive doll and now not a tower or turret of the castle was to be seen. "Oh!" groaned Peg Amy, "Ruggedo has done something dreadful with his Mixed Magic!"

Wag rubbed his eyes and looked all around. "Why, it's gone!" he cried, waving his paws. "What shall we do? If only we weren't so small!"

"We've got the magic box," said Peg hopefully, "and somehow I don't feel as small as I used to feel; do you?"

"Well, I feel pretty queer, myself," said the rabbit, twitching his nose. "Maybe it's because I'm hungry. There's a kitchen garden over there near the royal stables and I think if I had some carrots I'd feel better."

"Of course you would!" cried Peg, jumping up. "I forgot you had to eat." So, very cautiously they stole into the royal cook's garden. Wag had often helped himself to carrots from this garden before, but now sitting on his haunches he stared around in dazed surprise.

"Everything's different!" wailed the rabbit dismally. "You're the same and I'm the same but everything else is all mixed up. Look at this carrot. Why, it's no bigger than a blade of grass." Wag held up a carrot in disgust. "Why, it will take fifty of these to give me even a taste and the lettuce—look at it! Everything's shrunk, even the houses!" cried the big funny bunny, looking around. "My wocks and hoop soons, sheverything's hunk!"

Peg Amy had followed Wag's gaze and now she jumped up in great excitement. "I see it now!" cried Peg. "It's us, Wag. Everything's the same but we are different. Some of that Mixed Magic has made us grow. We're bigger and everything else is the same. I am as tall as the little girl who used to play with me and you are even bigger and I'm glad, because now we can help find the castle and Ruggedo and try to make everything right again."

Peg clasped her wooden hands. "Aren't you glad too, Wag?"

The rabbit shook his head. "It's going to take an awful lot to fill me up," he said doubtfully. "I'll have to eat about six times as much as I used to."

"Well, you're six times as large; isn't that any comfort?"

"My head doesn't feel right," insisted Wag. "As soon as I talk fast the words all come wrong."

"Maybe it didn't grow as fast as the rest of you," laughed the Wooden Doll. "But don't you care, Wag. I know what you mean and I think you're just splendid! Now hurry and finish your carrots so we can decide what to do.

"If Mixed Magic caused all this trouble," added Peg half to herself, "Mixed Magic's got to fix it. I'm going to look at that box." Wag, nibbling industriously, had not heard Peg's last speech or he would doubtless have taken to his heels.

Sitting unconcernedly in a cabbage bed, the Wooden Doll took the gold box from her pocket. Fortunately she had not snapped the magic snap and it opened quite easily. Her fingers were stiff and clumsy and the moon was the only light she had to see by, but it did not take Peg Amy long to realize the importance of Glegg's magic.

"I wonder if he rubbed this on the castle," she murmured, holding up the bottle of Vanishing Cream. "And how would one bring it back? Let me see, now." One after the other, she took out the bottles and boxes and the tiny tea set. The Re-animating Rays she passed over, without realizing they were responsible for bringing her to life, but the Question Box, Peg pounced upon with eager curiosity.

"Oh, if it only would answer questions!" fluttered Peg. Then, holding the box close to her mouth, she whispered, "Where is Ruggedo?"

"Who are you talking to?" asked Wag, looking up in alarm. "Now don't *you* get mixed up, Peg!"

"It's a Question Box," said the Wooden Doll, "but it's not working very well." She shook it vigorously and held it up so that the light streaming down from the stable window fell directly on it. In silver letters on the lid of the box was one word—Ev!

"Ev—Ruggedo's in Ev!" cried Peg Amy, rushing over to the rabbit. "Can you take me to Ev, Wag dear?"

"Of course," said Wag, nibbling faster and faster at his carrots. "I'll take you anywhere, Peg."

"Then it's going to be all right; I know it," chuckled the Wooden Doll, and putting all the magic appliances back into the box she closed the lid with a snap. And this time the magic catch caught.

"Is it far to Ev?" asked Peg Amy, looking thoughtfully at the place where the castle had once been.

"Quite a long journey," said Wag, "but we'll go a hopping. Ev is near Ruggedo's old home and it's across the Deadly Desert, but we'll get there somehow. Trust me. And when I do!" spluttered Wag, thumping his hind feet determinedly, "I'll pound his curly toes off—the wicked little monster!"

"Did you ask the Question Box where the castle was?" he inquired hastily, for he saw Peg was going to tell him he must not pound Ruggedo.

"Why, no! How silly of me!" Peg felt in her pocket and brought out the gold box. She tried to open it as she had done before but it was no use. She pulled and tugged and shook it. Then Wag tried.

"There's a secret to it," puffed the rabbit at last. "Took Rug a whole night and day to discover it. Can't you remember how you opened it before, Peg?"

The Wooden Doll shook her head sadly.

"Well, never mind," said Wag comfortingly. "Once we find Ruggedo we can make him tell. We'd better start right off, because if any of the people around here saw us they might try to capture us and put us in a circus. We are rather unusual, you know."

The rabbit regarded Peg Amy complacently. "One doesn't see six-foot rabbits and live dolls every day, even in Oz!"

"No," agreed Peg Amy slowly, "I s'pose not!"

The moon, looking down on the strange pair, ducked behind a cloud to hide her smile, for the giant funny bunny, strutting about pompously, and old-fashioned wooden Peg, in her torn frock, were enough to make anyone smile.

"You think of everything," sighed Peg, looking affectionately at Wag.

"Who wouldn't for a girl like you? You're a Princess, Peg—a regular Princess." The rabbit said it with conviction and again Peg happily smoothed her dress.

"Hop on," chuckled Wag, "and then I'll hop off."

Seating herself on his back and holding tight to one of his long ears, Peg announced herself ready. Then away through the night shot the giant bunny—away toward the western country of the Winkies—and each hop carried him twelve feet forward and sent up great spurts of dust behind.

Chapter 11
The King of The Illumi Nation

While Ruggedo was working all this mischief in the Emerald City, Pompadore and the Elegant Elephant had fallen into strange company. After the Prince's

49

disappearance, Kabumpo stared long and anxiously at the white marble stone with its mysterious inscription, "Knock before you fall in."

What would happen if he knocked, as the sign directed? Something upsetting, the Elegant Elephant was sure, else why had Pompa called for help?

Kabumpo groaned, for he was a luxurious beast and hated discomfort of any sort. As for falling *in*—the very thought of it made him shudder in every pound. But selfish and luxurious though he was, the Elegant Elephant loved Pompa with all his heart. After all, he had run off with the Prince and was responsible for his safety. If Pompa had fallen in he must fall in too. With a resigned sigh, Kabumpo felt in his pocket to see that his treasures were safe, straightened his robe and, taking one last long breath, rapped sharply on the marble stone with his trunk. Without a sound, the stone swung inward, and as Kabumpo was standing on it he shot headlong into a great black opening. There was a terrific rush of air and the slab swung back, catching as it did so the fluttering edge of the Elegant Elephant's robe of state. This halted his fall for about a second and then with a spluttering tear the silk fringe ripped loose and down plunged the Elegant Elephant, trunk over heels.

After the third somersault, Kabumpo, right side up, fortunately, struck a soft inclined slide, down which he shot like a scenic railway train.

"Great Grump!" coughed Kabumpo, holding his jeweled headpiece with his trunk. "Great—" Before he reached the second grump, his head struck the top of the passage with terrific force, and that was the last he remembered about his fall. How long he lay in an unconscious state the Elegant Elephant never knew. After what seemed several ages he became aware of a confused murmur. Footsteps seemed to be pattering all around him, but he was still too stunned to be curious.

"Nothing will make me get up," thought Kabumpo dully. "I'm going to lie here forever and—ever—and ever—and—" Just as he reached this drowsy conclusion, something red hot fell down his neck and a voice louder than all the rest shouted in his ear. "*What are you?*"

"Ouch!" screamed Kabumpo, now thoroughly aroused. He opened one eye and rolled over on his side. A tall, curious creature was bending over him. Its head was on fire and as Kabumpo blinked angrily another red hot shower spattered into his ear. With a trumpet of rage Kabumpo lunged to his feet. The hot-headed person fell over backwards and a crowd of similar creatures pattered off into the corner and regarded Kabumpo uneasily. They were as tall as Pompa but very thin and tube-like in shape and their heads appeared to be a mass of flickering flames.

"Like giant candles," reflected the Elegant Elephant, his curiosity getting the better of his anger. He glanced about hurriedly. He was in a huge white tiled chamber and the only lights came from the heads of its singular occupants. A little distance away Prince Pompadore sat rubbing first his knees and then his head.

"It's another faller," said one of the giant Candlemen to the other. "Two fallers in one day! This is exciting—an 'Ouch' it calls itself!"

"I don't care what it calls itself," answered the second Candleman crossly. "I call it mighty rude. How dare you blow out our king?" shouted the hot-headed fellow, shaking his fist at the Elegant Elephant. "Here, some of you, light him up!"

"Blow out your King?" gasped Kabumpo in amazement. Sure enough, he had. There at his feet lay the King of the Candles, stiff and lifeless and with never a head to bless himself with. While the Elegant Elephant stared at the long candlestick figure a fat little Candleman rushed forward and lit with his own head the small black wick sticking out of the King's collar.

Instantly the ruddy flame face of the King appeared, his eyes snapping dangerously. Jumping to his feet he advanced toward Pompadore. "Is this your Ouch?" spluttered the King, jerking his thumb at Kabumpo. "You must take him away at once. I never was so put out in my life. Me, the hand-dipped King of the whole Illumi Nation, to be blown out by a bumpy creature without any headlight. Where's *your* headlight?" he demanded fiercely, leaning over the Prince and dropping hot tallow down his neck.

Pompa jumped up in a hurry and backed toward Kabumpo. "Be careful how you talk to him," roared the Elegant Elephant, swaying backwards and forward like a big ship. "He's a Prince—the Prince of Pumperdink!" Kabumpo tossed his trunk threateningly.

"A Prince?" spluttered the King, changing his tone instantly. "Well, that's different. A Prince can fall in on us any time and welcome but an Ouch! Why bring this great clumsy Ouch along?" He rolled his eyes mournfully at Kabumpo.

"He's not an Ouch," explained Pompa, who was gradually recovering from the shock of his fall. "He is Kabumpo, an Elegant Elephant, and he blew you out by mistake. Didn't you, Kabumpo?"

"Purely an accident—nothing intentional, I assure you," chuckled Kabumpo. He was beginning to enjoy himself. "If there's any more trouble I'll blow 'em all out," he reflected comfortably, "for they're nothing but great big candles."

Seeing their King in friendly conversation with the strangers, the other Candlemen came closer—too close for comfort, in fact. They were always leaning over and dropping hot tallow on a body and the heat from their flaming heads was simply suffocating.

"Sing the National Air for them," said the Candle King carelessly and the Candlemen, in their queer crackling voices, sang the following song, swaying rhythmically to the tune:

"Flicker, flicker, Candlemen,
Cheer our King and cheer again!
Neat as wax and always bright,
Cheer's the King of candle light!
Kindle lightly—dwindle slightly,
Here we burn both day and nightly,
Here we have good times to burn
Till each one goes out in turn."

"Thank you," said Pompa, mopping his head with his silk handkerchief.

"Thank you very much," Kabumpo groaned plaintively, for the great elephant was nearly stifled.

"How is it you are so tall and thin?" asked Pompa after an awkward pause.

"How is it you are so short and lumpy and unevenly dipped?" responded King Cheer promptly. "If I were in your place," he gave Kabumpo a contemptuous glance, "I'd have myself redipped. Where are your wicks? And how can you walk about without being lighted?"

"We're not fireworks," puffed Kabumpo indignantly and then he gave a shrill scream. Ten Candlemen tottered and went out, falling to the ground with a great clatter. Then Pompa leaped several feet in the air and his scream put out five more.

"Stop!" cried King Cheer angrily. "Stand where you are!" But Kabumpo and Pompa neither stopped nor stood where they were. The Elegant Elephant rushed over to the Prince and threw his heavy robe over his head. And just in time, for Pompa's golden locks were a mass of flames. Then the Prince tore off his velvet jacket and clapped it to Kabumpo's tail, which also was blazing merrily.

"Great Grump!" rumbled the Elegant Elephant furiously, when he had extinguished Pompa and Pompa had extinguished him. "I'll put you all out for this!" He raised his trunk and pointed it straight at the Candlemen, who cowered in the far corner.

"I was only trying to light you up," wailed a little fellow, holding out his hands pleadingly. "I thought that was your wick." He pointed a trembling finger at Kabumpo's tail and another at Pompa's head.

"I was only trying to light you up," wailed the Candleman

"Wick!" snorted Kabumpo in a rage—while the Prince ran his hand sorrowfully through his one luxuriant pompadour, of which nothing but a short stubble remained—"Wick! What would we be doing with wicks?"

"I don't think he meant any harm," put in Pompadore, whose kind heart was touched by the little Candleman's terror. "And it wouldn't help us any."

"Thought it was my Wick," shrilled Kabumpo, glaring over his shoulder at his poor scorched tail. "He's a wick-ed little wretch. He's ruined your looks."

"I know!" Pompa sighed dismally. "No one will want to marry me now. It's all coming true, Kabumpo, just as Count It Up said. Remember? 'If a thin Prince sets out on a fat elephant to find a Proper Princess, how many yards of fringe will the elephant lose from his robe and how bald will the Prince be at the end of the journey?' And we've scarcely begun!"

"Great hay stacks!" whistled Kabumpo, his little eyes twinkling. "So I have lost every bit of fringe from my robe and my tail and half the back of my robe besides. This is nice, I must say."

"We only tried to give you a warm welcome," said the King timidly.

"Warm welcome! Well I should think you did," sniffed Kabumpo. "How do we get out of here?"

"Oh, that's very simple," said the King, cheering up. "Tommy, go for the Snuffer."

Before Kabumpo or Pompa realized what this would mean a little Candleman named Tommy Tallow had returned with a tall black candle person. He stepped to the side wall, quickly jerked a rope and down over Kabumpo dropped a great brass snuffer and over the Prince another.

"That ought to put the cross old things out," Pompa heard the King say just before his snuffer reached the floor.

"This is terrible," fumed the poor Prince, thumping on the sides of the huge brass dome. "I might as well have stayed at home and disappeared comfortably. My poor old father and my mother! I wonder where they are now?"

Sunk in gloomy reflection, Pompadore leaned against the side of the snuffer. And one cannot blame him for feeling dismal. The fall down the deep passage, the shock of losing his hair and now imprisonment under a stifling brass dome were enough to extinguish the hopes of the stoutest hearted adventurer.

"I shall never find a Proper Princess!" wailed Pompa, tying and untying his handkerchief. But just then there was a creak from without and the great dome lifted as suddenly as it had fallen—so suddenly in fact that Pompa fell flat on his back. There stood Kabumpo winding up the long rope with his trunk and grumbling furiously all the while.

"Takes more than a snuffer to keep me down," wheezed the Elegant Elephant, hurrying over and jerking the Prince to his feet. "Three humps of my shoulders and off she goes! What makes it so dark?"

"The Candlemen have all gone," sighed Pompa, brushing his hand wearily across his forehead. "All except that one."

In a distant corner sat Tommy Tallow and the light from his head was the only light in the great chamber. He was reading a book with tin leaves and looked up in surprise when he saw the Elegant Elephant and Pompadore approaching. Then he started to sputter and ran toward a bell rope at the side of the chamber.

"Stop!" shouted Kabumpo, "or I'll blow off your head!" At that the little Candleman trembled so violently that his flame head almost went out.

"Now suppose you show us the way out," snapped the Elegant Elephant, stamping one big foot until the floor trembled.

"You could burn out!" gasped Tommy faintly. "That's what we do!"

"Don't say out," whispered Pompa anxiously. "We want to go away from here," he explained earnestly. "Back on the top of the ground, you know."

"Oh!" whistled Tommy Tallow, his face lighting up. "That's easy—this way, please!" He almost ran to a big door at one side of the room and tugging it open, waved them through.

"Good-bye!" he called, slamming the door quickly behind them.

Kabumpo and the Prince found themselves in a wide dim hallway. It slanted up gradually and there were tall candle guards stationed about a hundred yards apart all of the way.

"Are you going to a birthday party or a wedding?" asked the first guard, as they passed him.

"Wedding," sniffed Kabumpo. "Why?"

"Well, hardly any of the candles go out of here unless they're needed for a birthday or a wedding," explained the guard, shifting his big feet. "You're mighty poorly made though. What kind of candles do you call yourselves?"

"Roman," chuckled Kabumpo with a wink. "We roam around," he added ponderously.

"Do all the candles used above ground come from here?" asked Pompa curiously.

"Certainly," replied the guard. "All candles come from Illumi—and they don't like to leave either because as soon as they strike the upper air they shrink down to ordinary cake and candlestick size. Distressing, isn't it?"

"I suppose it must be," smiled Pompadore. "Good-bye!" The guard touched his flame hat and Kabumpo quickened his pace.

"I want air," rumbled the great elephant, panting along as fast as he could go. "I've seen and felt about all I care to see and feel of the Illumi Nation."

"So have I!" The Prince of Pumperdink touched his scorched locks and sighed deeply. "I'm afraid Ozma will never marry me now, and Pumperdink will disappear forever!"

"Don't be a Gooch!" snapped the Elegant Elephant shortly. "Our adventures have only begun."

They passed the rest of the guards without further conversation, and after about two hours came to the end of the long tiled passageway and stepped upon firm ground again.

Kabumpo was terribly out of breath, for the whole way had been up hill. For a full minute he stood sniffing the fresh night air. Then, turning around, he looked for the opening through which they had come. Not a sign of the passage anywhere!

"That's curious," puffed the Elegant Elephant. "But never mind. We don't want to go back anyway."

"I should say not," gasped the Prince wearily. "Where are we now, Kabumpo?"

"Still in the Gilliken country, I think, but headed in the right direction. All we have to do is to keep going South," said the Elegant Elephant cheerfully.

"But we've had nothing to eat since morning," objected Pompadore.

"That's so," agreed Kabumpo, scratching his head thoughtfully, "and not a house in sight!"

"But I smell something cooking," insisted the Prince, sniffing hungrily.

"So do I," said the Elegant Elephant, lifting his trunk, "and it smells like soup. Let's follow our noses, Pompa, my boy."

"Yours is the longest," laughed the Prince, as Kabumpo swung him upon the elephant's back. So, guided by the fragrant whiffs that came floating toward them, Kabumpo set out through the trees.

Chapter 12
The Delicious Sea of Soup

"Strange that we don't see any houses," puffed Kabumpo, swinging along rapidly.

"I hear water," answered Pompa, peering out over Kabumpo's head, "and there it is!"

Rippling silver under the rays of the moon, which shone brightly, lay a great inland sea. The trees had thinned out, and a smooth, sandy beach stretched down to the shore. A slight mist hung in the air and all around was the delicious fragrance of vegetable soup.

"Somebody's making soup," sighed the Prince, "but who, and where?"

"Never mind, Pompa," wheezed the Elegant Elephant, walking down to the water's edge, "perhaps you can catch some fish, and while you cook them I'll go back and eat some leaves."

With a jerk of his trunk, Kabumpo pulled a length of the heavy silver thread from his torn robe and handed it up to Pompa. Fastening a jeweled pin to one end, the Prince cast his line far out into the waves. At the first tug he drew it in.

"What is it?" asked the Elegant Elephant, as Pompa pulled the dripping line over his trunk.

"Oh, how delicious! How wonderful!" exclaimed the once fastidious Prince of Pumperdink.

Kabumpo could hear him munching away with relish.

"What is it?" he asked again.

"A carrot! A lovely, red, delightful, tender carrot!"

"Carrot! Who ever heard of a sea carrot?" grunted Kabumpo. "I'm afraid you're not yourself, my boy. Let me see it."

Snaps and crunches, as Pompa consumed his strange catch, were the only answer, and in real alarm the Elegant Elephant moved away from the shore, and in doing so bumped against a white sign, stuck in the sand.

"Please Don't Fall In," directed the sign politely, "*It Spoils The Soup.*"

"Soup!" sputtered Kabumpo. Then another sign caught his eye: "*Soup Sea—Salted To Taste—Help Yourself.*"

"Come down—come down here directly!" cried the Elegant Elephant, snatching the Prince from his back. "Here's the soup—a whole sea full. Now all you need is a bowl."

Swallowing convulsively the last bit of carrot, Pompa stood staring out over the tossing, smoking soup sea. Every now and then a bone or a vegetable would bob out of the waves, and the poor hungry Prince of Pumperdink thought he had never seen a more lovely sight in his life.

"We'll probably be awarded a china medal for this," chuckled the Elegant Elephant. "Won't old Pumper's eyes stick out when we tell him about it? But now for a bowl!"

Swinging his trunk gently, Kabumpo walked up the white beach, and had not gone more than a dozen steps before he came to a cluster of huge shells. He turned one over curiously. "Why, it's a soup bowl," whistled the Elegant Elephant. He rushed back with it to Pompadore, who still stood dreamily surveying the soup.

"I never thought I'd be so thrilled by a common soup bowl," thought Kabumpo, staring at the Prince in amusement. He stepped out on a rock and dipped up a bowl of the hot liquid.

"Here! Drink!" commanded the Elegant Elephant, handing the bowl to the Prince. "Drink to the Proper Princess and the future Queen of Pumperdink."

"Don't go," begged the Prince between gulps, "I shall want two—three—several!"

Kabumpo laughed good naturedly. "This is the pleasantest thing that has happened to us. Here! Have another!"

Then both Pompa and the Elegant Elephant gasped, for out of the bubbling waves arose the most curious figure that they had ever seen—the most curious and the jolliest. He was made entirely of soup bones, and his head was a monster cabbage, with a soup bowl set jauntily on the side for a cap. For a cabbage head he sang very well and this was the song to which he kept time by waving a silver ladle:

"Ho! I am the King of the Soup Sea,
Yes, I am the King of the Deep;
My crown is a bowl and my sceptre a ladle,
I fell in the soup when I fell from the cradle,
And find it exceedingly cheap!
I stir it up nightly, and pepper it rightly—
A liquid perfection you'll find.
And here is a roll, sirs,
So fill up your bowl, sirs,
And think of me after you've dined."

When he came to "dined," the Soup King gave a playful leap and disappeared backward into the waves.

Pompa rubbed his eyes and looked at Kabumpo to see whether he had been dreaming.

"Oh!" cried Kabumpo, his eyes as round as little saucers. Floating gently toward them were two large, crisp, buttered rolls.

"The most charming King I've ever met," chuckled Kabumpo, scooping up the rolls and handing them to Pompa.

Pompa, staring dreamily ahead, first took a drink of soup, then a nibble of roll, too happy for speech. Four times the Elegant Elephant refilled the bowl. Then, his stomach full for the first time since they had left Pumperdink, the Prince stretched himself out on the sands.

"Now," puffed the Elegant Elephant ceremoniously, "if you think you've had quite enough, I'll snatch a few bites myself." Chuckling softly he made his way back to some young trees, and dined luxuriously off their tops.

When he returned to the beach, Pompa was fast asleep, and for a few moments Kabumpo was inclined to sleep himself. "But then," he reflected, "Ozma may require a lot of coaxing before she consents to marry Pompa, and two of our precious seven days are gone. It is plainly my duty to save Pumperdink. Besides, when Pompa is married he will be King of Oz! Then I, the Elegant Elephant, will be the biggest figure at Court."

Kabumpo threw up his trunk and trumpeted softly to the stars. Then, giving himself a big shake and a little stretch, he lifted the sleeping Prince to his back and started on again. In about two hours he had circled the Soup Sea and, guiding himself by a particularly bright and twinkling star, ran swiftly and steadily toward the South.

As the first streaks of dawn appeared in the sky, Kabumpo passed through a quaint little Gilliken village. He snatched a bag of rolls from a doorstep and stuck them into his pocket, but he did not stop, and so fast asleep was the little village that except for a few wideawake roosters, no one knew how important a person had passed through.

The sky grew pinker and pinker. You have no idea how pink the morning skies in Oz can be. Just as the sun got out of bed, the Elegant Elephant came to the wonderful Emerald City itself, shining and fairylike as a dream under the lovely colors of sunrise. Kabumpo paused and took a deep breath. Even he was impressed, and it took a good bit to impress him. He reached back and touched Pompa with his trunk.

"Wake up, my boy," whispered Kabumpo in a trembling voice. "Wake up and put on your crown, for we have come to the city of your Proper Princess."

Pompa sat up and rubbed his eyes in amazement. Without a word, he took the crown Kabumpo handed up to him, and set it on his scorched, golden head. Accustomed as Pompa was to grandeur, for Pumperdink is very magnificent in its funny old-fashioned way, he could not help but gasp at Ozma's fair city. The lovely green parks, the houses studded with countless emeralds, the shining marble streets, filled the Prince with wonder.

"I don't believe she'll ever marry me," he stuttered, beginning to feel quite frightened at his boldness.

"Nonsense," wheezed Kabumpo faintly. He was beginning to have misgivings himself. "Sit up now! Look your best, and I'll carry you straight into the palace gardens."

No one was awake. Even the Soldier with the Green Whiskers lay snoring against a tree, so that Kabumpo stole unobserved into the Royal Gardens.

"I don't see the palace," Whispered Pompa anxiously. "Wouldn't it show above the trees?"

"It ought to," said Kabumpo, wrinkling up his forehead. "But look! Who is that?"

Pompa's heart almost stopped, and even Kabumpo's gave a queer jump. On a golden bench, just ahead, sat the loveliest person either had seen in all of their eighteen birthdays.

"Ozma," gasped the Elegant Elephant, as soon as he had breath enough to whisper. "What luck! You must ask her at once."

"Not now," begged the Prince of Pumperdink, as Kabumpo unceremoniously helped him to the ground. His knees shook, his tongue stuck to the roof of his mouth. He had never proposed to a Fairy Princess before in his whole life. Then all at once he had an idea. Slipping his hand into the Elegant Elephant's pocket, he drew out the magic mirror. "I'll see if she's a princess," stuttered Pompa.

The elephant shook his head angrily but was afraid to speak again lest he disturb the quiet figure on the bench.

"And I'll not propose unless she is the one," said Pompa, tip-toeing toward the bench. Without making a sound he suddenly held the mirror before the startled and lovely lady.

"Glinda, good Sorceress of Oz," flashed the mirror promptly.

"Great gooseberries!" cried Glinda, springing to her feet in alarm and swinging around on Pompa. "Where did you come from?" After studying a whole day and night in her magic books, Glinda had returned to the Emerald City to try to perfect her plan for rescuing Ozma.

"From Pumperdink, your Highness," puffed Kabumpo, lunging forward anxiously. He, too, had seen the words in the mirror and the fear of offending a Sorceress made him quake in his skin—which was loose enough to quake in, dear knows!

"A thousand pardons!" cried the Prince, dropping on one knee and taking off his crown. "We were seeking Princess Ozma, the Fairy Ruler of Oz."

Glinda looked from Kabumpo to the Prince and controlled a desire to laugh. The Elegant Elephant's torn and scorched robe hung in rags from his shoulders and his jeweled headpiece was dangling over one ear. Pompa's clothes were equally shabby and his almost bald head with a lock sticking up here and there gave him a singular and comical appearance.

"Pumperdink?" mused Glinda, tapping her foot thoughtfully. Then, like a flash she remembered the entry in the Book of Records—"The Prince of Pumperdink is journeying toward the Emerald City."

"Why did you want to see Ozma?" asked Glinda anxiously. Perhaps these two strangers could throw some light on the mysterious disappearance of the Royal Palace.

"Our country was threatened with disappearance and I thought—"

"He thought Ozma might help us," finished the Elegant Elephant breathlessly. He did not believe in telling strange Sorceresses about everything. Now if Glinda had not been so occupied with the disappearance of the palace and all the dearest people in Oz, she might have been more curious about the disappearance of Pumperdink. As it was she just shook her head sadly. "I'm afraid Ozma cannot help you," she said, "for Ozma herself has disappeared—Ozma and everyone in the palace."

"Disappeared!" trumpeted the Elegant Elephant, sitting down with a thud. "Great Grump! The thing's getting to be a habit!"

What was to become of Pompa now? Would he never be King, nor he, Kabumpo, ever be known as the most Elegant Elephant in Oz? Had they made the long journey in vain?

"Where? When?" gasped Prince Pompadore.

"Night before last," explained Glinda. "I've been consulting my magic books ever since but have only been able to discover one fact."

"What is that?" asked Kabumpo faintly.

"That they are in Ev," said Glinda, "and that a giant carried them off. I came here early this morning to see whether I could discover anything new. Would you care to see where the castle stood?"

"Did he carry the castle off, too?" shuddered Pompa. Glinda nodded gloomily and led them over to the great hole in the center of the gardens.

For a minute she stood watching them. Then, glancing at a golden sun dial set in the center of a lovely flower bed, she murmured half to herself, "I must be off!" Next instant she clapped her hands and down swept a shining chariot drawn by white swans.

"Good-bye!" called Glinda, springing in lightly. "I'm off to Ev to try my magic against the giant's. Wait here and when I've helped Ozma perhaps I can help you!"

"Can't we help? Can't we go?" cried Pompa, running a few steps after the chariot, but Glinda, already high in the air, did not hear him and in the wink of an eye the chariot and its lovely occupant had melted into the pink morning clouds.

"Now what shall we do?" groaned the Prince, letting his arms drop heavily at his sides.

"Do!" snorted Kabumpo. "The thing for you to do is to act like a Prince instead of a Gooch! There are other ways of getting to Ev than by chariot."

The thought of Kabumpo in Glinda's chariot made Pompa smile in spite of himself.

"There! That's better," said the Elegant Elephant more pleasantly.

"Now, what's to hinder us from going to Ev and rescuing Princess Ozma? She couldn't help marrying you if you saved her from a giant, could she?"

"But could I save her—that's the question," muttered the Prince, looking uneasily at the yawning cavity where the castle had stood. "This giant must be a terrible fellow!"

"Pooh!" said Kabumpo airily. "Who's afraid of giants? I'll wind my trunk around his leg and pull him to earth. Then you can dispatch the villain. We must get you a sword, though," he added softly.

"All right! I'll do it!" cried the Prince, throwing out his chest. The very thought of killing a giant made him feel about ten feet high. "Do you know the way to Ev, Kabumpo? We'll have to hurry, because unless I marry Ozma before the seven days are up my poor old father and mother and all of Pumperdink will disappear forever."

You see, even Pompa had now got it into his head that Ozma was the Proper Princess mentioned in the scroll.

"We'll start at once," sighed the Elegant Elephant a bit ruefully. "I've had no sleep and precious little to eat but when you are King of Oz you can reward old Kabumpo as he deserves."

"Everything I have will be yours," cried the Prince, giving the elephant, or as much of him as he could grasp, a sudden hug. Then each took a long drink from one of the bubbling fountains and, munching the rolls Kabumpo had picked up in the Gilliken village, the two adventurers stole out of the gardens.

As they reached the gates, Kabumpo paused and his little eyes twinkled with delight. There lay the Soldier with the Green Whiskers, snoring tremendously and beside him was a long, sharp sword with an emerald handle. "Just what we need," chuckled

Kabumpo, snatching it up in his trunk. Then out through the gates and swiftly through the still sleeping city swept the Elegant Elephant and the Prince of Pumperdink, off to rescue Princess Ozma, a prisoner in Ev!

Chapter 13
On The Road To Ev

In their journey to Ev, Peg and Wag had a night's start of Kabumpo and Prince Pompadore, but towards morning Wag's ears began to droop with sleep.

"Gotta natch a sap, Peg," Wag muttered thickly, as they halted on a little hill.

"Natch a sap? Whats that?" asked the Wooden Doll anxiously. Wag made no answer—just flopped on his side and in a minute was asleep and snoring tremendously.

"Oh!" whispered Peg, pulling herself gently from beneath the sleeping rabbit. "He meant snatch a nap."

She laughed softly and seated herself under a small tree. The birds were beginning to waken and their singing filled Peg Amy with delight. "How wonderful it all is," she murmured, gazing up at the little ruffly pink clouds. "How wonderful it is to be alive!"

"Hello! Mr. Robin!" she called gaily, as a bird flew to a low bush beside her. "Are your children quite well?"

The robin swung backward and forward on his swaying branch; then burst into his best morning song.

"Oh!" cried Peg Amy, clasping her wooden hands, "I've heard that before! But how could I?" she reasoned, "I'm only a Wooden Doll and this is the first morning I have been alive. But then, how did I know it was a robin?"

Peg rubbed her wooden forehead in perplexity, for it was all very puzzling indeed. Below their little hill stretched the lovely land of the Winkies, with its great green forests and little yellow villages. The wind sent the leaves dancing above Peg's head and the early sunbeams made lovely patterns on the grass.

"I've seen it before!" gasped the Wooden Doll breathlessly. "The trees, the birds, the houses and everything!" Springing to her feet she ran awkwardly from bush to tree, touching the leaves and bending over the flowers as if they were old friends. Had it not been for the squeaking of her wooden joints, Peg would almost have forgotten she was a Wooden Doll, for at the sight of the lovely green growing things something warm and sunny seemed to waken in her stiff wooden breast. "I've been alive before," said Peg Amy over and over.

Suddenly, through the still morning air, came a loud, shrill laugh. Peg, who had been standing with her cheek pressed closely against a small tree, swung around quickly— so quickly in fact that she fell over and lay in a ridiculously bent double position before the new-comers.

It was Kabumpo and the Prince of Pumperdink. Traveling by the same road Wag had chosen but much more rapidly, the Elegant Elephant had come at sunrise to the little hill. He had been watching Peg for some time, and when he saw her dance awkwardly over to the tree, he could no longer restrain himself.

"Get out your mirror!" roared Kabumpo, shaking all over with mirth. "Here is your Proper Princess, Pompa, my boy—as royal a maiden as the country boasts. Ho, ho! Kerumph!"

"Don't be ridiculous," snapped Pompa, looking down curiously at the comical figure of Peg Amy.

"But she's so funny!" gasped Kabumpo, the tears rolling down his big cheeks.

"Who's funny?" demanded an angry voice and Wag, who had been awakened by Kabumpo's loud roars, hopped up, his ears quivering with rage.

"I'll pull your long nose for you!" cried Wag, advancing threateningly. "Don't you dare make fun of Peg. What are you, anyway?"

"Great Grump!" choked Kabumpo, without answering Wag's inquiry. "What kind of a rabbit is this?"

"A clawing, chawing, scratching kind—as you'll soon find out!" Wag drew himself up into a ball and prepared to launch himself at Kabumpo's head, when Peg straightened up and caught him by the ear.

"Don't, Wag, please," she begged. "He couldn't help laughing. I am funny. You know I am!" she sighed a bit ruefully.

"You're not funny to me," blustered Wag, still glaring at Kabumpo. "Who does he think he is?"

"I?" sniffed Kabumpo, spreading out his ears complacently, "I am the Elegant Elephant of Pumperdink. Notice my pearls; gaze upon my robe."

"You don't look very elegant to me," snorted Wag. "You look more like a tramp. Says he's a lelegant nelephant from Dumperpink," he whispered scornfully to Peg.

"And what's that you've got on your back?" he called, with a wave of his paw at Pompa. "A dunce?"

"Dunce!" screamed Kabumpo furiously. "This is the Prince of Pumperdink, you good-for-nothing lettuce-eater! What do you mean by laughing at royalty?"

"Royalty! Oh, ha, ha, ha!" roared Wag, rolling over and over in the grass. "But he's so funny!" He paused to take another look at the Prince. At this Kabumpo lunged forward, his eyes snapping angrily.

"Stop!" begged the Prince, tugging Kabumpo by the ear. "You were rude to his friend that—er—doll, so you must expect him to be rude to me. It's all your fault," he added reproachfully.

"Are you a Prince?" asked Peg Amy, staring up at Pompa with her round, painted eyes.

"Of course he's a Prince. Didn't I say so before? Who is that hoppy creature?"

"That's Wag—such a dear fellow." Peg smiled confidently at Kabumpo and he was suddenly ashamed of himself for laughing at her.

"Well, he needn't get waggish with me," grumbled the Elegant Elephant in a lower voice.

"Oh, don't quarrel!" begged Peg. "It's such a lovely morning and you both look so interesting."

Kabumpo eyed the big Wooden Doll attentively. It was smart of her to think him interesting. He cleared his throat gruffly.

"You're not as funny as you look," he admitted grandly, which was the nearest to an apology he had ever come. "But what are you doing here and why are you alive?"

"I don't know," explained Peg apologetically. "It just happened last night."

"It did? Well, where are you going?"

Wag still looked cross and his nose was twitching violently, but Peg politely answered Kabumpo's question.

"We're on our way to Ev to try to help Ozma," said the Wooden Doll, folding her hands quaintly.

"Why so are *we*!" cried Pompa, sliding down Kabumpo's trunk in a hurry.

"How do *you* expect to help her?" grunted Kabumpo, looking at Wag and Peg contemptuously.

"Don't mind him," begged Pompa, running up to Peg Amy. "Tell me everything you know about Ozma. Is she pretty?"

"Beautiful," breathed Peg, looking up at the sky. "Beautiful and lovely and good. That's why I want to help her."

"Then I sha'n't mind marrying her at all," said Pompa, with a great sigh of relief.

"Gooch!" roared Kabumpo angrily—"Telling everything you know!"

"Do you mean to say you think Ozma would marry *you*?" gasped Wag, sitting up with a jerk. "Oh, my wocks and hoop soons!" His ears crossed and uncrossed and with a final gurgle of disbelief Wag fell back on the grass.

"Well, is there anything so strange in that?" asked Pompa in a hurt voice. "I've *got* to marry her," he added, desperately appealing to Peg Amy. And while Kabumpo stood sulkily swinging his trunk the Prince told Peg the whole story of the magic scroll.

"I said you looked interesting," breathed Peg, as Pompa paused for breath. "Did you hear that, Wag? Unless he marries a Proper Princess in a proper time his whole Kingdom will disappear—his Kingdom and everyone in it!"

"But how do you know Ozma is the Proper Princess?" asked Wag, chewing a blade of grass. "The scroll didn't say Ozma, did it?"

"Kabumpo thinks Ozma is the Proper Princess," explained Pompadore, nodding toward the Elegant Elephant, "and he's usually right!"

"Humph!" sniffed Wag. "Well, maybe you are a Prince. You're not really bad looking if you had some fur on your head," he remarked more amiably. "What happened? Somebody pull it out?"

"Oh, Wag!" murmured Peg Amy, in a shocked voice.

"Burned off," sighed Pompa, and proceeded to tell of their fall into the Illumi Nation. He even told them about the Soup Sea and of their meeting with Glinda, the Good.

"Don't you care," said the big Wooden Doll, as Pompa mournfully rubbed his scorched head. "It will soon grow again and I don't see how Ozma could help loving you—you're so tall, and so polite." This kind little speech affected Pompa so deeply that he dropped on one knee and raised Peg's wooden hand to his lips.

"The creature has a lot of sense," mumbled Kabumpo, with his mouth full of leaves.

"Creature!" exclaimed Wag, sitting up straight and opening his eyes wide. "Her name is Peg Amy, Mr. Nelegant Lelephant."

"Oh, all right," sniffed Kabumpo hastily. "But you'll have to admit she's curious."

"Of course she is," said Wag complacently. "That's why I like her. She wasn't cut out to be a beauty, but to be companionable, and she is. When you've known Peg as long as I have"—Wag paused impressively—"you'll be proud to carry her on your back, Mr. Long Nose!"

"I've only known her a few minutes and I adore her!" said Pompa heartily. "Mistress Peg and I are good friends already." Peg curtseyed awkwardly. "I've done this before," she reflected curiously to herself.

"Shall we tell them about Ruggedo?" Peg asked aloud, turning to Wag.

"Yes, do!" begged Pompa. "Tell us something about yourselves. I never saw so large a rabbit in my life as Wag and as for *you*!"—Pompa paused, for Wag was eying him resentfully—"you are the largest, most delightful doll I have ever met, the only alive one, I might say. How did you know about Ozma's disappearance and how were you going to help her?"

"Mixed Magic!" whispered Wag, crossing his ears and his eyes as well. "Mixed Magic!"

"Magic?" gulped Kabumpo, swallowing a branch of sticky leaves whole. "Have *you* any magic?"

"A whole box full," sighed Peg Amy, patting her pocket softly.

"In that box is the magic that brought Peg to life!" shrilled Wag, pointing a trembling paw. "In that box is the magic that made us grow. In that box is the magic that caused Ozma's castle to disappear—!"

"In that box is the magic that brought Peg to life!" shrilled Wag

"Great Grump!" whistled Kabumpo. "How fortunate we fell in with them, Pompa." He held out his trunk. "Give me the box, my good girl, and you shall be fittingly rewarded when Pompa is King of Oz."

"That's a long time to wait," chuckled Wag, tickled by Kabumpo's outrageous impudence. "No, Peg and I will just keep the box, thank you."

"Of course you will," said Prince Pompadore, frowning at Kabumpo. "But as we are both bound on the same errand, let us travel together. Kabumpo and I are going to kill the giant who ran off with the castle."

The Prince held up his long sword. "And if you can help us, I shall thank you from the bottom of my heart." Pompa stretched out his hand impulsively.

"Well, that's more like," said Wag, pulling his ear thoughtfully. "And four heads are better than two!"

"Of course we'll help you!" cried Peg Amy. "The trouble is, we don't know ourselves how to open the magic box, but we do know that Ruggedo is in Ev and when we get there we will make him open the box and undo all this mischief."

"You mentioned him before," said Kabumpo, holding up his trunk. "Who is Ruggedo and what has he to do with Ozma?"

"Ruggedo is a wicked little gnome," explained Peg Amy gravely. "He used to be King of the Gnomes but he was banished from his Kingdom and Ozma gave him a little cottage in the Emerald City. He pretended to live there, but instead he tunneled a cave right underneath the palace. Wag helped him dig." Peg waved her hand at the rabbit. "And he was the only one who would stay with him. Then Ruggedo stole me. I was only a small, unalive doll, belonging to Trot, a little girl who lives with Ozma. Ruggedo stole me just to shake," continued Peg shuddering.

"That's why I'm going to pound his curly toes off!" screamed Wag, beginning to hop about at the very thought of Ruggedo.

"But how did you come to be so large and alive?" asked Kabumpo, who was growing more interested.

"Well, one night"—Peg dropped her voice to a whisper—"One night Ruggedo found this box of Mixed Magic hidden in the cave and then—"

"Then," screamed Wag hoarsely, "in some way we don't understand, Peg and I grew big, Peg came alive, the top blew off the cave—and depend upon it, whatever's happened to Ozma and her palace happened from something in that box. It's all Ruggedo's fault. When I catch him"—Wag began to wiggle his nose and paw his whiskers—"my wocks and hoop soons! I'll pound his curly toes off."

"And I'll help you!" cried Kabumpo heartily. He could not help but admire such spirit. "Come on—let's start. You may ride on my back with Pompa if you care to," finished the Elegant Elephant with a sidelong glance at Peg.

"Oh, thank you," smiled the Wooden Doll, "but Wag will carry me."

"I always carry Peg," said Wag jealously. "I've known her the longest."

"Oh, all right," sniffed Kabumpo, lifting Pompa up, "but if she ever *wants* to ride on my back she may."

"Humph!" grunted Wag, as the Wooden Doll settled herself on his shoulders. "Isn't he generous!"

Peg pulled down one of Wag's long ears. "It was kindly meant," whispered the Wooden Doll merrily.

"Ready?" puffed Kabumpo, backing out into the road. "We've no time to lose, for if we lose time we lose our Kingdom too. Forward for Pumperdink!"

"All right!" cried Wag, giving a great leap. "Follow me!" And off hopped the giant bunny so fast that Kabumpo had to stretch his legs even to keep him in sight.

Chapter 14
Terror In Ozma's Palace

Meanwhile strange things had been happening in Ozma's palace. For the people inside it had been a very mean time indeed. During Ruggedo's run to the mountains of Ev, they had almost been shaken out of their wits and when he sat down upon the mountain top there was not a person nor piece of furniture standing in the whole palace. Courtiers and servants who were not knocked senseless lay shaking in their beds or huddled in corners and under sofas and chairs, just as they had fallen when the first terrible crash lifted the palace into the air.

Ozma's four poster bed had collapsed, pinning the little Fairy Princess under a mass of silk hangings and curtain poles. Being a fairy, Ozma was unhurt, but not being able to move, nor to reach her Magic Belt or even make herself heard, she was forced to lie perfectly still and wait for help.

In Dorothy's sitting room there was not a sound but the ticking of the Copper Man's machinery. Trot and Betsy Bobbin had knocked their heads together so smartly that they were unconscious. Sir Hokus had been hurled violently against Tik Tok and the poor Knight had known nothing since. Dorothy lay quietly beside him, an ugly bruise on her forehead, where the emerald clock had landed.

"Scraps!" called the Scarecrow, sometime after the rumble and tumble had ceased, "are you there?"

"No, here!" gasped the Patch Work Girl, sitting up cautiously. She had bounced all around the room and finally rolled into a corner quite close to the Scarecrow himself. She put out her cotton hand as she spoke and touched him.

"How fortunate we are unbreakable," said the Scarecrow, pressing her cotton fingers convulsively and trying to peer out through the intense blackness of the room. "What happened?"

"Earthquake!" shivered Scraps. "And maybe it's not over!"

"Must have knocked everybody silly," said the Scarecrow huskily.

"Except us," giggled the Patch Work Girl. "We couldn't be knocked silly 'cause we were silly in the first place."

"Now, don't make jokes, please," begged the Scarecrow. "This is serious. Besides, I want to think."

"All right," said Scraps cheerfully. "I don't—but I'm going to feel around and see if I can find the matches. There used to be some candles on the mantel and—" As she spoke, Scraps fell headlong over Sir Hokus of Pokes and as luck would have it her cotton fingers closed over a small gold match box. Picking herself up carefully, Scraps struck a match on Sir Hokus' armor and looked anxiously around the room.

"They need water," said the Patch Work Girl, wrinkling up her patchwork forehead.

"So will you if you don't blow out that match!" cried the Scarecrow in alarm, for Scraps continued to hold the match till it burned to the very end. He jumped up clumsily and puffed out the light just in time. Scraps promptly lit another and as she did so the Scarecrow saw a tall blue candle sticking out of the waste basket.

"Here," said the Straw Man nervously. "Light this and stand it on the mantel there." By the flickering candle light the Scarecrow and Scraps tried to set Dorothy's room to rights. They dragged the mattress from the bed-room and placed the little girls on it, side by side. Sir Hokus was too heavy to move, so they merely loosened his armor and put a sofa cushion under his head. Then, just as Scraps was going for some water, the room began to tremble again.

"I told you it wasn't over," cried Scraps, flinging both arms about the Scarecrow's neck. And as they rocked to and fro she shouted merrily:

"Shaker! Shaker! Who art thee,
To shake a castle like a tree?
Shaker! Shaker! Go away
And come again some other day!"

"Now, Scraps," begged the Scarecrow, steadying the Patch Work Girl with one hand and catching hold of a table with the other, "everything depends on us. Do try to keep your head!"

"Keep my head!" shrilled Scraps, as the room tilted over and slid all the furniture sideways. "I'll be lucky if I keep my feet. Whoopee! Here we go!" And go they did with a rush into the farthest corner. Slowly the room righted itself and everything grew quiet again.

"I know what I'm going to do," said the Scarecrow determinedly. "Before anything else happens I'm going to see what has happened already."

"How?" asked Scraps, bouncing to her feet.

Dorothy and Toto

"The Magic Picture," gasped the Scarecrow. "You bring the candle, Scraps, like a good girl. You're less liable to take fire than I am. Then we'll come back and help Dorothy and the others."

"Good idea," said Scraps, taking the candle from the mantel. Breathlessly the two tip-toed along the hall to Ozma's apartment. On the wall in one of Ozma's rooms hangs the most magic possession in Oz. It is a picture representing a country scene, but when you ask it where a certain person is, immediately he is shown in the picture and also what he is doing at the time.

"So," murmured the Scarecrow, as they gained the room in safety, "if it tells where other people are, it ought to tell us where we are ourselves."

Drawing aside the curtain that covered the picture the Scarecrow demanded loudly, "Where are we?"

Scraps held the candle so that its flickering rays fell directly on the picture. Then both jumped in earnest, for in a flash the face of Ruggedo, the wicked old gnome King, appeared, on his head a great, green towering sort of hat.

The Scarecrow seized the candle from Scraps and held it closer to the picture. He squinted up one eye and almost rubbed his painted nose off.

"Great Kinkajous!" spluttered the Straw Man distractedly. "That's a palace on his head—an Emerald palace—Ozma's palace!"

"But how?" asked Scraps, her suspender button eyes almost dropping out. "He's nothing but a gnome. He's—"

Before Scraps could finish her sentence the palace began to tilt forward and they both fell upon their faces. Then the picture jerked loose and fell with a clattering slam on their heads, followed by such ornaments as had not already tumbled down before. Through it all Scraps held the candle high in air and fortunately it did not go out, despite the turmoil.

In a few moments the palace stopped rocking and a muffled call from Ozma sent the Scarecrow and Scraps hurrying to her bedside. After some trouble, for they were both flimsily made, they managed to free the little Princess of Oz from the poles and bed curtains.

"Goodness!" sighed Ozma, looking around at the terrible confusion.

"Not goodness, but badness," said the Scarecrow, settling his hat firmly, "and Ruggedo is at the bottom of it and of us." He quickly explained to Ozma what he had seen in the Magic Picture.

Slipping on a silk robe, Ozma followed them into the next room. When the picture had been rehung, they all looked again. This time Ozma asked where the palace was. Immediately the old Gnome King appeared and there could be no mistake—the palace was set squarely on his head. The picture did not show the real size of Ruggedo nor of the palace, but it was enough.

"He must have sprung into a giant," gasped Ozma, scarcely believing her eyes. "Oh, what shall we do?"

"The first thing to do is to keep him quiet. Every time he shakes his head it tumbles us about so," complained the Scarecrow, plumping up the straw in his chest. "And we must look after Dorothy and Betsy and Trot."

"And Sir Hokus," added the Patch Work Girl, flinging out one hand. "He's yearning to slay a giant. 'Way for the Giant Killer!'"

Without waiting for the others Scraps ran back to Dorothy's sitting room. Lighting another candle, for all the lights in the palace were out, Ozma and the Scarecrow followed.

"Odds Goblins!" gasped the Knight, as they entered. He was sitting up with one hand to his head.

"Not goblins—giants!" cried the Patch Work Girl, with a bounce, while Ozma ran for some water to restore her three little friends.

"Where?" puffed the Knight, lurching to his feet.

"Beneath you," said the Scarecrow, clutching at a wisp of straw that stuck out of his head. "Say! Some one wind up Tik Tok. There's a lot of thinking to be done here and his head works very well, even if it has wheels inside."

Sir Hokus, though still a bit dizzy, hastened to wind up all the Copper Man's keys. "Thanks," said Tik Tok immediately. "Give me a lift up, Ho-kus." The Knight obligingly helped the Copper Man to his feet. Then both stared in amazement at the topsy turvy room. Even in the dim candle light they could see that something very serious had occurred.

Jack Pumpkinhead picked himself up out of a corner, looking very much dazed.

Jack Pumpkinhead

Just then Dorothy opened her eyes, and Betsy and Trot, spluttering from the water the Patch Work Girl was pouring on their heads, sat up and wanted to know what had happened. In a few words Ozma told them what the magic picture had revealed.

"Ruggedo to a giant's grown
And set us on his head.
We've made some headway, you'll admit,
Since we have gone to bed!"

—shouted Scraps, who was growing more and more excited.

"Rug-ge-do will nev-er re-form," ticked the Copper Man sadly.

"But what are we going to do?" wailed Dorothy. "Suppose he leans over and spills us all out?"

"I shall take my sword," said Sir Hokus, speaking very determinedly, and backing toward the window as he spoke, "climb down, and slay the villain." He threw one leg over the sill.

"Come back!" cried Ozma. "Dear Sir Hokus, don't you realize that if you kill Ruggedo he will fall down and break us to pieces? Besides, wicked as he is, I could not have him killed."

"Yes, we should be all broken up if you did that," sighed the Scarecrow. "We must try something else."

Reluctantly, the Knight dropped back into the room. "Close the windows," ordered Ozma with a little shudder.

"I've thought of a plan," said Tik Tok, in his slow, painstaking way. "A ve-ry good plan."

"Tell us what it is," begged Dorothy. "And Oh, Tik Tok, hurry!"

"Eggs," said the Copper Man solemnly.

"Oh!" gasped Dorothy, "I remember. Eggs are the only things in Oz that Ruggedo is afraid of; for if an egg touches a gnome he shrivels up and disappears."

"Then where are the eggs?" demanded Sir Hokus gloomily. "In faith, this sounds more like an omelet than a battle. But if we're to fight with eggs instead of swords, let us draw them at once."

"You mean throw them," corrected Dorothy. But Tik Tok shook his head violently.

"Not throw them," said the Copper Man slowly, "threat-en to throw them."

"But how can we threaten a giant so far below us?" asked Ozma.

"Print a sign," directed Tik Tok calmly, "and low-er it down to him."

"Tik Tok," cried the Scarecrow, rushing forward and embracing him impulsively, "your patent-action-double-guaranteed brains are marvels. I couldn't have thought up a better plan myself."

Now off ran Scraps to fetch a huge piece of cardboard, and the Scarecrow for a paint brush, and Sir Hokus for a piece of rope.

"It's growing lighter," quavered Trot, looking toward the windows. The sky was turning gray with little streaks of pink, and the three girls huddled together on the mattress gave a sigh of relief; for nothing, not even a giant, seems so bad by daylight.

"Perhaps someone has already started to help us," said Ozma hopefully. "But here's the sign board. What shall we write?"

"How shall I begin?" asked the Scarecrow, dipping the brush into a can of green paint. "Dear Ruggedo?"

"I should say not," said Dorothy indignantly.

"Then I shall simply say, Sir," said the Scarecrow.

"If you move or turn or shake your head a-gain, ten thou-sand eggs will be hurl-ed from the pal-ace windows," suggested Tik Tok.

As this message met with general approval, the Scarecrow set it down with many flourishes and blotches of paint spilled between. Then Ozma painted her name and the Royal seal of Oz at the end.

Meanwhile, with the help of a pair of field glasses, Sir Hokus had located Ruggedo's nose, sticking out like a huge cliff below the middle window of Dorothy's room. So, tying a long rope to each corner of the sign, and rolling it up so it would go through the window, the Knight let it down till it dangled directly in front of Ruggedo's nose.

At first Ruggedo did not even see the sign, which was about as large as the tiniest visiting card—compared to him. But it blew against his face and tickled his cheek. He tried to brush it away. Then, suddenly noticing it was dangling from above, he seized it in one hand and held it close to his left eye. The words were so small for a giant that Ruggedo had to squint fearfully before he could make them out at all, but when he did he gave a bloodcurdling scream, and began to tremble violently.

"Ruggedo gave a bloodcurdling scream and began to tremble violently"

Up in the palace the entire company fell over and twenty windows were shaken to bits. Then everything grew quiet and there was perfect silence; for Ruggedo, realizing his danger, grew rigid with fright. Giant drops of perspiration trickled down his forehead. How long could he keep from moving?

"Well," said Dorothy after a few minutes had passed, "I guess that will keep him quiet, but what next? Shall we let ourselves down with ropes?"

"We have none long enough," said Sir Hokus.

"Then I'll fall out and go for help," said the Scarecrow brightly, and started toward the window. When he reached it he paused in astonishment. "Look," he cried, waving excitedly to the others, "here comes someone, walking right over the clouds."

73

Chapter 15
The Sand Man Takes a Hand

Someone was coming toward the palace. A little gray-cloaked old gentleman—a surprisingly quick and nimble old gentleman—springing from cloud to cloud and pausing now and then to straighten a huge sack he carried over his left shoulder. He was so busy admiring the lovely sky colors behind him and waving merrily at the fluffy cloud figures above his head, that he did not see Ozma's shining palace until he was almost upon it.

"Stars!" murmured the little old gentleman, balancing perilously on the very edge of a silver cloud. "Another air castle! How delightful! I shall jump right through it!"

Gathering himself together he leaped straight toward the window out of which Dorothy and Ozma and the others were looking. With a soft thud he struck the emerald setting just above the window, and down tumbled his sack, opening as it fell and filling the air with clouds of silver sand. Down tumbled the little old gentleman, turning over and over, and finally landing on a blankety white cloud far below.

All of this Dorothy saw, and was about to ask Ozma what it could mean when an overpowering drowsiness stole over her. Before she could speak her eyes closed, and she sank backward into a big arm chair. Trot and Betsy Bobbin with two little sighs crumpled down to the floor. The head of Sir Hokus dropped heavily on the sill, and not even in Pokes had he snored so lustily. Ozma slipped gently down beside Betsy and Trot, and in a moment there was not a person awake in that whole big palace. Even the little mice in the kitchen were fast asleep, with heads on their paws.

Did I say everyone? Well, not quite everyone had fallen under the strange spell. Tik Tok, Scraps, and the Scarecrow, who had never slept in their lives, were still wide awake, and regarding their companions with astonishment and alarm. The Tin Woodman was taking things calmly, oiling up his joints and polishing his tin jacket with silver polish.

"This is no time to sleep," cried the Scarecrow, shaking Sir Hokus. "I say—wake up!" But all their efforts to arouse their companions were in vain.

"En-chant-ment," said the Copper Man. "Some—" With a click and a whirr Tik Tok's machinery ran down, and as Scraps and the Scarecrow were too upset to think of winding him, he stood as silent and dumb as the rest.

"What shall we do?" cried the Scarecrow, seizing Scraps' arm. "Jump out of the window and go for help, or stay here and guard the palace?"

Scraps looked out of the window. "Stay here," shuddered the Patch Work Girl, drawing in her head quickly.

"Then," said the Scarecrow, "let us arm ourselves and prepare to withstand any attack." He snatched up a pair of fire tongs and Scraps grasped the poker. Falling into step, the two marched from the top to the bottom of the palace. Everywhere the same sight met their gaze; rooms turned topsy turvy, and spread over floors and sofas and chairs the sleeping figures of Ozma's once lively Courtiers and servants. The effect was so distressing that Scraps and the Scarecrow found themselves whispering and treading about on tip-toe. After inspecting the whole palace they returned to Dorothy's room and placed themselves disconsolately in the doorway.

"Anyway, Ruggedo is quiet," sighed the Scarecrow, "and that is something." Scraps started to make a verse, but the silence and the ghostlike atmosphere of the sleeping palace had dashed even the spirits of the Patch Work Girl and she subsided with an indistinct mumble.

Ruggedo was silent for a very good reason. Ruggedo was asleep, too—asleep sitting up as stiff as a stone image, for even in his sleep he dreamed of the dreaded bombardment of eggs.

All this had happened because the little man in gray had taken Ozma's palace for an air castle, and who could blame him for that? Even the Sand Man would not expect to find a regular palace set among the clouds. There are plenty of dream castles, to be sure, and one of the Sand Man's chief delights is to jump through them and admire their lovely furniture. But sure-enough castles—the little fellow could not get over it. Sitting cross-legged on the white cloud, which floated close to Ruggedo's head, he stared and stared.

The Tin Woodman, oiling up his joints

"Well, I never," chuckled the Sand Man, and turned a somersault for very amazement. Then, not knowing what else to do or think, he sensibly decided to hurry home and tell the whole affair to his wife. His empty bag he found on a tall treetop, and without one backward glance he bounded into the air and disappeared. Really, it was quite lucky the little old gentleman spilled his bag of sand where he did, for the only safe giant is a sleeping giant, and while Ozma and her friends lay dreaming they could not worry.

"Will they sleep forever?" sighed Scraps, after she and the Scarecrow had sat silently for an hour.

"Seems likely," said the Scarecrow gloomily. "But even if they do," he plucked three straws from his chest, "we shall stick to our post to the very end."

The Scarecrow regarded the sleeping figures of the little girls affectionately.

"To the end of forever?" gulped Scraps, putting her cotton finger in her mouth. "How long is that?"

"That," said the Scarecrow resignedly and settling himself comfortably, "that is what we shall soon see."

Chapter 16
Kabumpo Vanquishes The Twigs

"Do you think you were alive before?" asked Kabumpo, squinting down his long trunk at Peg Amy. She had begged him to take off his plush robe and, spreading it on the grass, was beating it briskly with the branch of a tree.

"Yes," sighed the Wooden Doll, pausing with uplifted stick and regarding Kabumpo solemnly, "I must have been alive before 'cause I keep remembering things."

"What kind of things?" asked the Elegant Elephant, rubbing himself lazily against a tree.

"Well, this for instance," said Peg, holding up a corner of the purple plush robe. "I once had a dress of it. I'm sure I had a dress of this stuff."

"When you were a little doll?" asked Kabumpo curiously.

"No," said Peg, giving the robe a few little shakes, "before that. And I remember this country, too, and the sun and the wind and the sky. If I'd only been alive one day I wouldn't remember them, would I?"

"Queer things happen in Oz," said Kabumpo comfortably. "But why bother? You are alive and very jolly. You are traveling with the most Elegant Elephant in Oz and in the company of a Prince. Isn't that enough?"

Peg Amy did not reply but kept on beating the plush robe with determined little thumps and staring off through the trees with a very puzzled expression in her painted blue eyes. They had traveled swiftly all morning through the fertile farmlands of the Winkies and had paused for lunch in this little grove. Peg, not needing food, and Kabumpo, finding plenty of tender branches handy, had remained together while Wag and the Prince sought more nourishing fare. Many a little Winkie farmer had stared in amazement as Peg and Pompa passed that morning but so fast did Kabumpo and Wag travel that before the Winkies were half sure of what they had seen there was nothing but a cloud of dust to wonder over and exclaim about.

"If you had a pair of scissors, I could cut off the burned part of your robe and make it more tidy," said Peg, when she had finished beating the dust out of Kabumpo's gorgeous blanket.

"There might be a pair in my pocket," said the Elegant Elephant. "Here, let me get them," he added hastily. "For suppose she should look into the Magic Mirror," he thought suddenly. "It might tell her something terrible!"

Even in this short time Kabumpo had grown fond of queer wooden Peg and careless as he was somehow he did not want to hurt her feelings again. Sure enough, there was a pair of silver scissors in with the jewels he had tumbled into his pocket before leaving Pumperdink. So Peg carefully cut away all the scorched part of Kabumpo's robe and pinned under the rough edges with three beautiful pearl pins.

"Now lift me up into that small tree and I'll drop it over you," she laughed gaily. This Kabumpo did quite easily and after Peg Amy had smoothed and adjusted the robe, she crept out on the end of the branch and straightened the Elegant Elephant's pearl head dress and brushed all the dust from his forehead with a handful of damp leaves.

"You're a good girl, Peg," said Kabumpo, sighing with contentment. "I don't care whether you never were alive before or not, you've more sense than some people who've lived for centuries. I'm going to give that gnome something on my own account. Dared to shake you, did he? Well, wait till I get through shaking him!"

"It didn't hurt," said Peg reflectively, "but it ruined all my clothes. Do you think Prince Pompadore minds having me look so shabby?"

Kabumpo shifted about uneasily. "Will this help?" he asked sheepishly, pulling a lovely pearl necklace from his pocket. "Ozma doesn't need everything," he muttered to himself.

"Oh! How perfectly pomiferous!" cried Peg. "Lift me down so I can try it on." In a trice Kabumpo swung her down from the tree and awkwardly Peg Amy clasped the chain about her wooden neck. Then she flung both arms round Kabumpo's trunk. "You're the biggest darling old elephant in Oz!" cried Peg happily.

Kabumpo blinked. He was accustomed to being called elegant and magnificent but no one—not even Pompa—had ever called him an old darling before and he found he liked it immensely.

While Peg ran to look at her reflection in a small pool he resolved to get the Wooden Doll a position at Court, for, in spite of her stiff fingers, Peg was very deft and clever. "And she shall have a purple plush dress too," said Kabumpo grandly.

Just then Pompa and Wag returned in a high good humor. The Prince had tapped on the door of a small farm house and the little Winkie lady had been most hospitable. Not only had she given the Prince all he could eat, but she had allowed Wag to go into the garden and pick two dozen of her best cabbages. His size had greatly astonished her and she had insisted upon measuring him twice with her yellow tape measure but finally, without revealing the purpose of their journey, the two managed to get away. As all were now refreshed and rested, they decided to start on again.

"We ought to reach Ev by evening," puffed Wag, between hops.

"But I wish we could open the Magic Box," sighed Peg, holding on to Wag's ear, "for in that box there's Flying Fluid!"

"We'd make a remarkably nice lot of birds," chuckled Kabumpo, looking over his shoulder, "now wouldn't we?"

"You would," laughed Pompa. "What else was in the box, Peg?"

It was hard to talk while they were being jolted along, but Peg, being of wood, did not feel the bumps and Pompa, being a Prince, pretended not to, so that they continued their conversation in jerky sentences.

"There's Vanishing Cream, a little tea kettle and some kind of rays and a Question Box," said Peg, holding up her wooden hand. "A Question Box that answers any question you ask it."

"There is!" exclaimed Kabumpo, stopping short. "Well, I wish we could ask it whether Pumperdink has disappeared."

"And how to rescue Ozma, and who sent the scroll!" cried Pompa. "Oh, do let me try to open it, Peg!"

So Peg handed over Glegg's Magic Box and as they pounded along the Prince tried to pry it open with his pearl pen knife. "It would save us such a lot of trouble," he murmured, holding it up and screwing his eye to the keyhole.

"Better let it alone," advised Wag, wiggling his ears nervously. "Suppose you should grow as big for you as I am for me. Suppose you should explode or vanish!"

"Vanish!" coughed Kabumpo. "Great Grump! Put it away, Pompa. Wait till we reach Ev and make that wicked little Ruggedo open it for us. Who is this Glegg, anyway?"

"A lawless magician, I guess," said Wag, "or he wouldn't have owned a box of Mixed Magic. Ozma doesn't allow anyone to practice magic, you know."

"Why, I'll bet he was the person who sent the scroll!" exclaimed the Prince suddenly. "Don't you remember, Kabumpo, it was signed J. G.?"

"Not a doubt in the world," rumbled Kabumpo. "I'll throw him up a tree when I catch him and Ruggedo, too!"

"Oh, please don't," begged Peg Amy. "Perhaps they are sorry."

"Not half as sorry as they will be," wheezed Kabumpo, plowing ahead through the long grass like a big ferryboat under full steam.

Wag hopped close behind and Peg kept her eyes fixed upon Pompa's back. In spite of his scorched head, he seemed to Peg the most delightful Prince imaginable.

"I'll brush off his cloak and cut his hair all evenly," thought Peg. "Then, perhaps Ozma will say *yes* when he tells her his story and asks for her hand. But I wonder what will become of me," Peg sighed ever so softly and looked down with distaste at her wooden hands and torn old dress. Nothing very exciting could happen to a shabby Wooden Doll.

"Why, I haven't even any right to be alive," she reflected sadly. "I'm only meant to be funny. Well, never mind! Perhaps I can help Pompa and maybe that's why I was brought to life."

This thought, and the gleam of the lovely pearls Kabumpo had given her, so cheered Peg that she began to hum a queer, squeaky little song. The country was growing rougher and more hilly every minute. The sunny farmlands lay far behind them now and as Peg finished her song they came to the edge of a queer, dead-looking forest. The trees were dry and without leaves and there were quantities of stiff bushes and short stunted little trees standing under the taller ones.

Peg had an odd feeling that hundreds of eyes were staring out at them but the forest was so dim that she couldn't be sure. There was not a sound but the crackling of the dead branches under Wag's and Kabumpo's feet.

"I don't like this," choked Wag. "My wocks and hoop soons! What a pleerful chase!"

"It isn't very cheerful," shivered Peg. "Oh, look, Wag! That big tree has eyes!" At Peg's remark the tree doubled up its branches into fists and stepped right out in front of them. At the same instant all the other trees and bushes moved closer, with dry crackling steps.

"Now we have you!" snapped the tallest tree in a dreadful voice.

"Now we have you!" snapped the tallest tree in a dreadful voice

"Now we have you!" crackled all the other skitter-witchy creatures, crowding closer.

"Pigs, pigs, we're the twigs;
We'll tweak your ears and snatch your wigs!"

they shouted all together. One taller than the rest leaned over and seized Wag by the ear with its twisted fingers.

"Help!" screamed Wag, kicking out with his hind legs. Immediately Kabumpo began laying about with his trunk.

"Stand back!" he trumpeted angrily, "or I'll trample you to splinters."

Pompa stood up on Kabumpo's back and began to wave his sword threateningly. At this the ugly creatures grew simply furious. They snatched at the Prince with their long, claw-like branches, tearing at his sadly scorched hair and almost upsetting him.

"Stop! Stop!" cried Peg Amy, waving her wooden arms frantically. "Don't hit him. He's going to be married. Hit me, I'm only made of wood!"

"Don't you dare hit her!" shrilled Pompa, slicing off the branch head of the nearest Twig. "I am a Prince and she is under my protection. Don't touch her!"

By this time Kabumpo had cleared himself a space ahead and Wag a space behind. Every time Kabumpo's trunk flew out, a dozen of the queer crackly Bushmen tumbled over forward and every time Wag's heels flew out a dozen crumpled over backward. Pompa kept his sword whirling and, after several had lost top branches, the whole crowd fell back and began grumbling together.

"Now then!" puffed Kabumpo angrily, "let's make a dash for it, Wag. Come on; we'll smash them to kindling wood!"

"What's all this commotion?" cried a loud voice. The Twigs fell back immediately and a bent and twisted old tree hobbled forward.

"Strangers, your Woodjesty," whispered a tall Twig, waving a branch at Kabumpo.

"Well, have you pinched them?" asked the King in a bored voice.

"A little," admitted the tall Twig nervously, "but they object to it, your Woodjesty."

"Well, what if they do?" rasped the King tartly. "Don't be gormish Faggots. You know I detest gormishness. It seems to me you might allow my people a little innocent diversion," he grumbled, turning to Pompa, "they don't get much pleasure!"

"Pleasure!" gasped the Prince, while Kabumpo and Wag were so astonished that they forgot to fight.

"What does he mean by gormish?" whispered Peg uneasily to Wag. Before he could answer, the Twigs, who evidently had decided not to be gormish, made a rush upon the travelers. But Kabumpo was ready for them with uplifted trunk. With a furious trumpet he charged straight into the middle, Wag at his heels, with the result that the Twigs went crackling and snapping to the ground in heaps.

"All we need is a match," grunted Kabumpo, pounding along unmindful of the scratching and clawing. "They're good for nothing but kindling wood."

"Don't be gormish," he screeched scornfully, as he flung the last Twig out of his way and Wag and he never stopped till they had put a good mile between themselves and the disagreeable pinchers.

"Are you hurt?" asked Kabumpo, stopping at last and looking around at Pompa. "If we keep on this way you won't be fit to be seen—much less to marry. Let's have a look at you." He lifted the Prince down carefully and eyed him with consternation. The Prince had seven long scratches on his cheek and his velvet cloak was torn to ribbons.

"I declare," spluttered the Elegant Elephant explosively, "you're a perfect fright. I declare, it's a grumpy shame!"

"Well, don't be gormish," said the Prince, smiling faintly and wiping his cheek with his handkerchief.

"Let me help," begged Peg Amy, falling off Wag's back. "Ozma won't mind a few scratches and what do clothes matter? Anyone would know he was a Prince," she added, taking Pompa's cloak and regarding it ruefully.

Pompa smiled at Peg's earnestness and made her his best bow but Kabumpo still looked anxious. "Everyone's not so smart as you, Peg," he sighed gloomily. "But come along. The main thing is to rescue Ozma and after that perhaps she won't notice your scratches and torn cloak. She'll think you got them fighting the giant," he finished more hopefully.

With a few more of Kabumpo's jeweled pins Peg repaired Pompa's cloak. Then, after tying up Wag's ear, which was badly torn, they started off again.

"What worries me," said Wag, twitching his nose very fast, "what worries me is crossing the Deadly Desert. We're almost to it, you know."

"Never cross deserts till you come to 'em," grunted Kabumpo, with a wink at Peg Amy.

"Oh, all right," sniffed Wag, "but don't be gormish. You know how I detest gormishness!"

While Pompa and Peg were laughing over these last remarks a most terrible rumble sounded behind them.

"Now what?" trumpeted Kabumpo, turning about.

"Sheverything's mixed hup!" gulped Wag, putting back his ears. "Hold on to me, Peg!"

Chapter 17
Meeting The Runaway Country

Everything was mixed up, indeed. Moving toward the little party of rescuers was a huge jagged piece of land, running along on ten tremendous feet and feeling its way with its long wiggly peninsula. The feet raised it several yards above the ground.

"If we crouch down maybe it will run over us," panted Pompa, sliding down Kabumpo's trunk.

"I don't want to be run over," shrilled Wag, beginning to hop in a frenzied circle.

"Stop!" cried the Land in a loud voice, as Wag and Kabumpo started to run.

"Better stop," puffed Kabumpo, his eyes rolling wildly, "or it'll probably fall on us." Trembling in spite of themselves, they stood still and waited for the Land to approach.

"I've often heard of sailors hailing land with joy," gulped Wag, "but this—well, how did it get this way?"

As the Runaway Country drew nearer, its peninsula fairly quivered with excitement and as it reached them it pulled up its front feet and tilted forward to get a better view. Its eyes were two small blue lakes and its mouth a broad bubbling river.

"I claim you by right of discovery," cried the Land in its loud, river voice and before they could make any objection it scooped them up neatly and tossed them on a little hill.

"This is outrageous," spluttered the Elegant Elephant, picking Peg out of some bushes. "We've been kidnapped!"

"Let's jump off!" cried Wag, beginning to hop toward the edge.

"I wouldn't do that," said the Land calmly, "because I'd only run after you again. You might as well settle down and grow up with me. I'm not such a bad little Country," it added quietly, "just a bit rough and uncultivated."

"Well, what's that got to do with us," demanded Kabumpo, staring the Country right in its lake-eyes. "We're on an important mission and we haven't time for this sort of thing at all."

"It's a matter of saving a Princess," cried Pompa impulsively. "Couldn't you, please—"

"Let someone else save her," said the Country indifferently, beginning to move off sideways like a crab. "You're the first savages I've found and I'm going to keep you. Not that you're what I'd pick out," it continued ungraciously. "That wooden girl looks uncommonly odd and you two beasts are even queerer. But I'm liberal, I am, and the boy looks all right so far as I can see."

"But, look here," panted Wag, twitching his nose very fast, "this is all wrong. Land is supposed to stand still, isn't it? You've no right to discover us. We don't want to be discovered. Put us off at once—do you hear?"

"Yes, I hear," said the Runaway Country gruffly. "And I've heard about enough. Don't anger me," it shrilled warningly. "Remember, I'm a wild, rough Country."

"You're the wildest Country I ever saw," groaned the Elegant Elephant, falling up against a tree. "And of all ridiculous happenings this is the worst!"

"Never mind," whispered Peg Amy, standing on her tip toes to whisper in Kabumpo's huge ear, "it's taking us in the right direction, and maybe, if we were very polite—?"

"Go ahead and try it," wheezed Kabumpo, rolling his eyes. "I'm too upset." He hugged the tree again.

So Peg climbed to the top of the little hill and, waving her wooden arms to attract the Country's attention, called cheerfully:

"Yoho, Mr. Land! Where are you going?"

At first the Land only blinked his blue lake-eyes sulkily but, as Peg paid no attention to his ill temper and began making him pretty compliments on his mountains and trees, he gradually cheered up.

"I'm going to be an island," he announced finally. "That's where I'm going. I'm tired of being a hot, dry old undiscovered plateau and I don't intend to stop till I come to the Nonestic Ocean."

"Oh!" groaned Wag, falling over backwards. "We're going to be cast away on a desert island."

Peg held up a warning finger. "What made you want to run away and be an island?" she asked faintly for, even to Peg, things looked serious.

"Well," began the Land, giving itself a hitch, "I lay patiently for years and years waiting to be discovered. Nobody came—not even one little missionary. I kept getting lonelier and lonelier. You see how broken up I am!"

"Yes, we can see that, all right," sniffed Kabumpo.

"And I'm ambitious," continued the Country huskily. "I want to be cultivated and built up like other Kingdoms. So, one day I made up my mind I wouldn't wait any longer but would run off myself and discover some settlers. As I have ten mountains and each has a foot there seemed to be no reason why I shouldn't run away, so I *did*—and I *have!*"

The Country rolled its lakes triumphantly at the little party on the hill. "I have found some settlers and I'm looking to you to develop me into a good, modern, up-to-Oz Kingdom. I'm a progressive Country and I expect you to improve and make something out of me," it continued earnestly. "There's gold to be dug out of my mountains, plenty of good farm land to be planted and cities to be built, and—"

"What do you think we are?" exploded Kabumpo indignantly. "Slaves?"

"He'll get used to it in time," said the Runaway Country, paying no attention to Kabumpo, "and he'll be useful for drawing logs. Now you," he turned his watery eyes full on Peg Amy, "you seem to be the most sensible one in the party, so I think I shall bestow myself upon you. Of course you're not at all handsome nor regular, but from now on you may consider yourself a Princess and *me* as your Kingdom."

"Thank you! Thank you very much!" said Peg Amy, hardly knowing what else to say.

"Hurrah for the Princess of Runaway Island!" cried Wag, standing on his head. "I always knew you were a Princess, Peg my dear."

"Oh, hush!" whispered Pompa. "Can't you see it's getting more reasonable? Maybe Peg can persuade it to stop."

"If it doesn't stop soon I'll tear all its trees out by the roots," grumbled Kabumpo under his breath. "Logging, indeed! Great Grump! Here's the Deadly Desert!"

The air was now so hot and choking that Pompa flung himself face down on the cool grass. The Runaway Country did not seem to notice the burning sands and pattered smoothly along on its ten mountain feet.

"Something has to be done, quick," breathed Peg, clasping her hands, "for soon we'll be in Ev."

Pompa, holding his silk handkerchief before his face, had come up beside her and they both looked anxiously for the first signs of the country that held Ruggedo and the giant who had run off with Ozma's palace.

"Oh, Mr. Land," called Peg suddenly.

"Yes, Princess," answered the Country, without slackening its speed.

"Have you thought about feeding us?" asked the Wooden Doll gently. "I don't see any fruit trees or vegetables or chickens and settlers must eat, you know. We ought to have some seeds to plant and some building materials, oughtn't we, if we're going to make you into an up-to-Oz Country?"

"Pshaw!" said the Runaway Country, stopping with a jolt, "I never thought of that. Can't you eat grass and fish? There's fine fish in my lakes."

"Well, I don't eat at all," explained Peg pleasantly, "but Pompa is a Prince and a Prince has to have meat and vegetables and puddings on Sunday—"

"And I have to have lettuce and carrots and cabbages, or I won't work!" cried Wag, thumping with his hind feet and winking at Kabumpo. "I'll not dig a single mountain!"

"And I've got to have my ton of hay a day, too!" trumpeted the Elegant Elephant, "or I'll not lug a single log. Pretty poor sort of a Country you are, expecting us to live on grass as if we were donkeys and goats."

The Runaway Country rolled its lakes helplessly from one to the other. "I thought settlers always managed to get a living off the land," it murmured in a troubled voice.

"Not us!" rumbled Kabumpo. "Not enough pie in pioneer to suit this party!"

"Has your Highness anything to suggest?" asked the Country, looking anxiously at Peg.

"Well," said the Wooden Doll slowly, "suppose we stop at the first country we come to and stock up. We could get a few chickens and seeds and saws and hammers and things."

"You'd run away," said the Runaway Country suspiciously. "Not but what I trust you, Princess," he added hastily, "but them." He scowled darkly at Kabumpo and Wag. "I'll not let them out of my sight."

"How our little floating island loves us," chuckled Wag, nudging the Elegant Elephant.

"They won't run away," said Peg softly. "And if they did you could easily catch them again."

"That's so; I'll stop wherever you say," sighed the Country, starting on again.

"What are you going to do?" whispered Pompa, catching Peg's arm.

"I don't know," said Peg honestly, "but perhaps if we can make it stop something will turn up. We're almost across the desert now and that's a big help."

"You're wonderful!" cried Pompa, eying Peg gratefully. "How can I ever thank you?"

"Better get your sword ready," said Peg practically, "for we may run into that giant any minute now." Even Kabumpo and Wag had stopped making jokes and were straining their eyes toward Ev.

"Let's all stand together!" gasped Wag breathlessly. Before Peg or Pompa had time to plan, or Kabumpo to reply, the Runaway Country stepped off the desert and swept over the border and into the Kingdom of Ev, making straight for a tall purple mountain.

"Do you see anything that looks like a giant, or a palace?" asked Peg, leaning forward.

"Oh, help!" screamed Wag just then, while Kabumpo gave an earsplitting trumpet. Peg grasped Pompa and Pompa clutched Peg and no wonder! Directly in front of them were the legs and feet of the most terrible and tremendous giant they had ever imagined. He was sitting on the mountain itself and only a part of him was visible, for his head and shoulders were lost in the clouds.

Kabumpo gave an ear-splitting trumpet

"What's the matter? What's the matter?" rumbled the Runaway Country, tilting forward slightly so it could see. One look was enough. With a frightened jump, that sent the four travelers hurtling through the air, it began running backwards and in a moment was out of sight.

Peg was the first to recover her senses. Being wood, bumps didn't bother her. She rose stiffly and gazed around her. Pompa's feet were waving feebly from a small clump of bushes. Kabumpo stood swaying near by, while Wag lay over on his side with closed eyes.

"Oh, you poor dears!" murmured Peg, and running over to the bushes she pulled out the Prince of Pumperdink and settled him with his back against a tree. He was much shaken by his high dive from the island, but pulled himself together and patted Peg's wooden hand kindly. By this time Kabumpo had gotten his bearings and came wabbling over.

"You've got a black eye, I see," wheezed the Elegant Elephant bitterly.

"Not so very black," said Peg cheerfully. "Are you hurt, Kabumpo?"

The Elegant Elephant felt himself all over with his trunk. "Well, I'm not used to being flung about like a bean bag," he said irritably. Then he lowered his voice hastily, as he caught another glimpse of those dreadful giant feet. "I'll go help Wag," he whispered, backing away quickly.

It took some time to rouse the giant rabbit, but finally he opened his eyes. "I shought I thaw a giant," he muttered thickly. "Hush!" warned Kabumpo. "He's over there." He waved his trunk in the direction of the mountain and began dragging Wag firmly away.

"C'mon over here," he called in a loud whisper to Peg and Pompa. Leaning heavily on Peg Amy the Prince came. Then he gave a cry of distress. "My sword!" he gasped, staring around a bit wildly.

"I'll find it," said Peg obligingly. "You sit still and rest."

"Where's the Magic Box?" coughed Kabumpo, with an uneasy glance in the giant's direction.

Now that they were actually in Ev, the Elegant Elephant began to doubt the wisdom of his plan for killing the monster.

"Gone!" wailed Pompa, feeling in his pocket. "I dropped it when I fell off the Land. What shall we do, Kabumpo?"

"Don't be a Gooch," gulped the Elegant Elephant, but he said it without spirit.

"It's probably around here somewhere." Moving quietly, Kabumpo began to poke about with his trunk.

Just then Peg Amy came flying toward them, her ragged dress fluttering in the breeze.

"Look!" whispered the Wooden Doll, dropping on her knees before them.

In her hands was Glegg's Box of Mixed Magic and *it was open*!

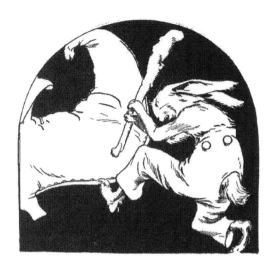

Chapter 18
Prince Pompadore Proposes

While Peg and Pompa and the Elegant Elephant eyed the box, Wag, twitching his nose and mumbling very fast under his breath, backed rapidly away. He was not going to run the risk of any more explosions. So anxious was the big rabbit to put a good distance between himself and Glegg's Mixed Magic, that he never realized that he was backing toward the giant till a sharp thump on the back of the head brought him up short.

Trembling in every hair, Wag looked over his shoulder. *Stars!* He had run into the terrible, five-toed foot of the giant himself. At first Wag was too terrified to move. But suddenly the hair on the back of his neck bristled erect. He peered at the giant's foot more attentively. His eyes snapped and, seizing a stout stick that lay near by, he brought it down with all his might on the giant's toes.

"It's Ruggedo!" screamed Wag, hopping up and down with rage. "And I'll pound his curly toes off. I don't care if he is a giant! I'll pound his curly toes off!"

The stick whistled through the air and whacked the giant's toes again.

Now of course we have known all along that the giant was Ruggedo, but it was a great surprise for the rescuers. Ruggedo was bad enough to deal with as a gnome— but a giant Ruggedo! *Horrors!*

"Stop him! Stop him!" cried Peg Amy, throwing up her hands and scattering the contents of the box of magic in every direction.

"What are you trying to do?" roared Kabumpo, plunging forward. "Get us all trampled on?"

A muffled cry came down from the clouds and, as Kabumpo dragged Wag back by the ear, something flashed through the air and bounced upon the Elegant Elephant's head.

"It's the Scarecrow!" chattered Wag, wriggling from beneath Kabumpo's trunk. Kabumpo opened his eyes and peered down at the limp bundle at his feet. As he looked the bundle began to pull itself together. It sat up awkwardly and began clutching itself into shape.

"Where'd you come from?" gasped the Elegant Elephant. Without speaking, the Scarecrow waved his hand upward and rose unsteadily to his feet. Then, catching sight of Peg Amy and Pompadore, the Straw Man bowed politely. Meanwhile Wag, seeing that Kabumpo's attention was diverted, began to sidle back toward Ruggedo.

"Stop!" cried the Scarecrow, running after him. "Are you crazy? Don't you know Ozma's palace is on his head? Every time he moves everyone in the palace tumbles about. Was it you who stirred him up and made him spill me out of the window?"

"I'll wake him up some more, the wicked old scrabble-scratch," muttered Wag, but Kabumpo jerked him back roughly.

The Scarecrow waved his hand upward

"Great Grump!" choked the Elegant Elephant, shaking Wag in his exasperation. "Here we've come all this way to save Princess Ozma and now you want to upset everything."

"That's the way to do it," said the Scarecrow, rolling his eyes wildly.

"Please stop it, Wag," begged Peg Amy, throwing her wooden arms around the big rabbit's neck, and as Pompa added his voice to Peg's, Wag finally threw down his stick.

"Who is that beautiful girl?" asked the Scarecrow of Kabumpo. The Elegant Elephant looked at the Straw Man sharply, to see that he was not poking fun at the Wooden Doll. Finding he was quite serious, he said proudly, "That's Peg Amy, the best little body in Oz. She's under my protection," he added grandly.

Just then Pompa and Peg came over and Wag, who had often seen the Scarecrow in the Emerald City, introduced them all.

"Did I understand you to say you had come to rescue Ozma?" asked the Scarecrow, who could not keep his eyes off the Elegant Elephant.

"Did I understand you to say Ozma's palace was on Ruggedo's head?" shuddered Kabumpo, glancing fearfully in the direction of the mountain.

The Scarecrow nodded vigorously and told in a few words of their terrible journey to Ev and their present perilous position. How the palace had gotten on Ruggedo's head, he admitted was a puzzle to him. Kabumpo and Pompadore listened with amazement, especially to the part where they had threatened Ruggedo with eggs.

"And he's kept still for two days just on account of eggs?" gasped the Elegant Elephant incredulously.

"Well, no," admitted the Scarecrow, wrinkling up his forehead. "A little man came flying through the air the first morning and bumped into the palace and instantly everyone except Scraps and me fell asleep. Ruggedo was put to sleep, too; we could hear him snoring."

"Why, it must have been the Sand Man," breathed Peg Amy. "I have heard he lived near here."

"Are they asleep now?" asked Pompa, clutching the Scarecrow's arm. How romantic—thought the Prince of Pumperdink—to rescue and waken a sleeping Princess!

But the Scarecrow shook his head. "A few minutes before I fell out they began to wake up and I'd just gone to the window to look for Glinda when Ruggedo gave a howl and ducked his head and here I fell." The Scarecrow spread his hands eloquently and smiled at Peg.

"Has Glinda been here?" asked Kabumpo jealously.

"Yes," said the Scarecrow. "She came this morning and she's been trying all sorts of magic to reduce Ruggedo without harm to the palace."

"Great Grump! Do you hear that?" Kabumpo rolled his eyes anxiously toward the Prince. "If Glinda's magic takes effect before ours then where'll we be? Peg! Peg! Where's the box of Mixed Magic?"

"Would you mind telling me," burst out the Scarecrow, who had been examining one after another in the party with a puzzled expression, "would you mind telling me how you happened to know about the palace disappearing; how you got across the sandy desert; how you expect to help us; how he (with a jerk at Wag) came to be too large; how she (with a jerk of his thumb at Peg) came to be alive; and—"

"All in good time; all in good time!" trumpeted Kabumpo testily. "You sound like the Curious Cottabus! The principal thing to do now is to save Ozma. Will Ruggedo stay quiet a little longer?"

"If he's not disturbed," said the Scarecrow, with a meaning glance at Wag.

"Well, my hocks and woop soons!" cried the rabbit indignantly. "Isn't anyone going to punish him? He shook and shook Peg and he meddled with magic and blew up into a giant. He's run off with the palace. Doesn't he deserve a pounding?"

"Friend," said the Scarecrow, "I admire your spirit but my excellent brains tell me that this is a case where an ounce of prevention is worth a pound of cure. But have we the ounce of prevention?"

"Here's the Question Box," announced Peg, who had run off at Kabumpo's first call. "What shall we ask it first?"

"How to save the lovely Princess of Oz," spoke up Pompa, running his hand over his scorched locks. "Where's my crown, Kabumpo?"

Kabumpo fished the crown from his pocket and Pompa set it gravely upon his head as Peg asked the Question Box:

"How shall we save the lovely Princess of Oz?"

These maneuvers so astonished the Scarecrow that he lost his balance and fell flat on his nose. When he recovered Peg was clapping her wooden hands and Kabumpo was dancing on three legs.

"You're as good as married, my boy!" cried Kabumpo, thumping the Prince upon the back.

"What is it? What's happened?" gasped the Scarecrow.

"Why, the Question Box says to pour three drops of Trick Tea on Ruggedo's left foot and two on his right and he will then march back to the Emerald City, descend into his cave and, after the palace has settled firmly on its foundations, he will shrink down to his former size," read Peg Amy, holding the Question Box close to her eyes, for the printing was very small.

"Hurrah!" cried the Scarecrow, throwing up his hat. "Peggy, put the kettle on and we'll all have some tea! But where'd you get all this magic stuff?" he asked immediately after.

"Out of a box of Mixed Magic," puffed Kabumpo, his little eyes twinkling with anticipation as he watched Peg. First she filled the tiny kettle at a near-by brook; then she lit the little lamp and dropped some of the Trick Tea into the kettle. Bright pink clouds arose from the kettle, as soon as Peg had set it over the flame, and while they waited for it to boil Pompa put another question.

"Has Pumperdink disappeared?" asked the Prince, in a trembling voice.

"N-o," spelled the Question Box slowly, and Kabumpo settled back with a great sigh of relief.

"I told you everything would be all right if you followed my advice," said the Elegant Elephant. "Stand up now and try to forget your black eye. You are the Prince of Pumperdink and I am the Elegant Elephant of Oz."

"But why all the ceremony?" asked the Scarecrow, looking mystified.

Kabumpo only chuckled to himself and, as the Trick Tea was now ready, Peg took the little kettle and began to tip-toe toward Ruggedo.

"I hope it's red hot," grumbled Wag resentfully. "He's getting off easy, the old scrabble-scratch! Getting off! Say, look here!" He gestured violently to Kabumpo. "If Ruggedo returns to the Emerald City with the palace on his head, where does Pompa come in?" He pointed a trembling paw at the Prince, his nose twitching so fast it made the Scarecrow blink.

"Stop!" trumpeted the Elegant Elephant, plunging after Peg Amy. He reached her just in time.

"I'm no better than Pumper," grunted Kabumpo, mopping his brow with the tail of his robe. "Suppose, after all our hardships, I had allowed Ozma and the palace to get away without giving Pompa a chance to ask her—"

"But we ought to save her as quick as we can," ventured Peg. "Couldn't we hurry back to the Emerald City again?"

"It might be too late," wheezed Kabumpo. "Let—me—see!"

"Hello!" cried the Scarecrow. "Here comes Glinda." As he spoke the swan chariot of the good Sorceress floated down beside the little party.

"Bother!" groaned Kabumpo, as Glinda stepped out.

"Some strangers," called the Scarecrow, gleefully running toward Glinda, "some strangers with a box of Mixed Magic trying to help."

"If we could have a few words with Ozma," put in the Elegant Elephant hastily, "everything would be all right."

Glinda looked at Kabumpo gravely. "It's unlawful to practice magic. You must know that," said the Sorceress sternly.

"But it's not our magic, your Highness," explained Peg Amy, setting down the little kettle. "We found it, and we're only trying to help Ozma."

"Well, in that case," Glinda could not help smiling at the Wooden Doll's quaint appearance, "I shall be glad to assist you, as all of my magic has proved useless."

"Aren't you the Prince of Pumperdink?" she asked, nodding toward Pompa. The Prince bowed in his most princely fashion and assured her that he was and, after a few hasty explanations, Glinda promised to bring Ozma down in her chariot.

"Tell her," trumpeted Kabumpo impressively, as the chariot rose in the air, "tell her that a young Prince waits below!"

While Pompa was still looking after Glinda's chariot, Peg Amy came up to him and extended both her wooden hands.

"I wish you much happiness, Pompa dear," said the Wooden Doll in a low voice.

Pompa pressed Peg's hands gratefully. "If it hadn't been for you I'd never have succeeded. You shall have everything you wish for now, Peg. Why, where are you going?"

"Good-bye!" called Peg Amy, trying to keep her voice as cheerful as her painted face, and before anyone could stop her she began to run toward a little grove of trees.

"Come back!" cried the Prince, starting after her.

"Come back!" trumpeted Kabumpo in alarm.

"I'll get her!" coughed Wag, hopping forward jealously. "I've known her the longest."

Pompa and Kabumpo both started to run, too, but just at that minute down swooped the chariot and out jumped Ozma, the lovely little Ruler of Oz.

"At last!" gasped Kabumpo, pushing Pompa forward.

If Ozma was startled by their singular appearance, she was too polite to say so, and she returned Pompa's deep bow with a still deeper curtsey.

"Glinda tells me you have come a long, long way just to help me," said Ozma anxiously. "Is that so?"

"Princess!" cried Pompa, falling on his knee. "I know you are worried about your palace and your Courtiers and your friends. Two drops of that Triple Trick Tea (he waved at the small kettle) upon Ruggedo's right foot and three on his left will set everything right!"

"But where did you get it—and why?" Ozma looked doubtfully at the Scarecrow.

"Might as well try it," advised the Scarecrow.

"We will explain everything later," puffed the Elegant Elephant. "Trust old Kabumpo, your Highness, and everything will turn out happily."

"I believe I will," smiled Ozma. "Will you try the Trick Tea, Glinda?"

Glinda took the kettle and poured it exactly as directed. First Ruggedo gave a gusty sigh that blew the clouds about in every direction.

"Look out!" warned Glinda.

Next instant they all fluttered down like a pack of cards, for Ruggedo had taken a step—a giant step that shook the earth as if it had been a block of jelly—and when they had picked themselves up Ruggedo was out of sight, tramping like a giant in a dream, back toward the Emerald City.

Ruggedo, tramping like a giant in a dream, back to the Emerald City

"You wait here!" cried Glinda to Ozma. "And I'll follow him!" She sprang into her chariot.

"How do you know he'll go back?" asked the little Ruler of Oz, staring with straining eyes for a glimpse of the giant.

"Because the Question Box said so," chuckled Kabumpo triumphantly.

"Good magic!" approved the Scarecrow. "But where is that charming Peg? I think I'll run find her."

No sooner had the Scarecrow disappeared than Pompa, swallowing very hard, again approached Ozma. But Ozma, still looking after Glinda's vanishing chariot, was hardly aware of the Prince of Pumperdink.

Poor Pompa dropped on his knee (which had a large hole in it by this time) and began mumbling indistinct sentences. Then, as Kabumpo frowned with disgust, the Prince burst out desperately, "Princess, will you marry me?"

"Marry you?" gasped the little Ruler of Oz. "Good gracious, *no!*"

Chapter 19
Ozma Takes Things In Hand

Prince Pompadore jumped up quickly.

"I told you she wouldn't!" he choked, looking reproachfully at Kabumpo. "I'm not half good enough."

"He doesn't always look so scratched up and Shabby," wheezed Kabumpo breathlessly. "We've been scorched and pinched and kidnapped. We've been through every kind of hardship to save your Highness—and *now!*" The Elegant Elephant slouched against a tree, the picture of discouragement. He seemed to have forgotten the jewels that were to have won the Princess for Pompa and his threat of running off with her should she refuse him.

"Why, you don't even know me," cried Ozma, dismayed by even the thought of marrying; for though the little Ruler of Oz has lived almost a thousand years she is no older than *you* are and would no more think of marrying than Dorothy or Betsy Bobbin or Trot. Ruling the Kingdom of Oz takes almost all of Ozma's time and in any that is left she wants to play and enjoy herself like any other sensible little girl. For Ozma is only a little girl fairy after all.

"I'm not going to marry anybody!" she declared stoutly. Then, because she really was touched by Pompa's woebegone appearance, she asked more kindly, "Why did you want to marry me especially?"

"Because you are the properest Princess in Oz," groaned the Prince, leaning disconsolately against Kabumpo. "Because if we don't Pumperdink will disappear and my poor old father and my mother and everyone."

"Not to speak of us," gulped the Elegant Elephant.

"But where is Pumperdink, and who said it would disappear?" asked Ozma in amazement. "And how did you happen to have this Trick Tea and come to rescue me?"

"The Prince always rescues the Princess he intends to marry," said Kabumpo wearily. "I should think you'd know that."

"Well, I'm very grateful, and I'll do anything I can except marry you," exclaimed Ozma, who was beginning to feel very much interested in this strange pair.

"Thank you," said Kabumpo stiffly, for he was deeply offended. "Thank you, but we must be going. Come along, Pompa."

"Don't be a Gooch!" This time it was Pompa who spoke. "I'm going to tell her everything!"

And Pompa, being as I have told you before the most charming Prince in the world, made Ozma a comfortable throne of green boughs and, throwing himself at her feet, poured out the whole story of their adventures, beginning with the birthday party and the mysterious scroll. He told of their meeting with Peg Amy and Wag and ended up with the ride upon the Runaway Country.

Kabumpo stood by, swaying sulkily. He was very much disappointed in the Princess of Oz. He felt that she had no proper appreciation of his or Pompa's importance.

"I'm going to find Peg," he called finally. "She's got more sense than any of you," he wheezed under his breath as he swept grandly out of sight.

Ozma put both hands to her head as Pompa finished his recital and really it was enough to puzzle any fairy. Scrolls, live Wooden Dolls, a giant rabbit, a mysterious magician threatening disappearances and Ruggedo's wicked use of the box of Mixed Magic.

"Goodness!" cried the little Ruler of Oz. "I wish the Scarecrow would come back. He's so clever I'm sure he could help us; but first you had better bring me the magic box."

Pompa rose slowly and, picking up all the little flasks and boxes that had spilled out when Wag pounded Ruggedo, he put them back into the casket and handed it to Ozma. She examined the contents as curiously as the others had done. The Expanding Extract was the only thing missing, for Ruggedo had poured the whole bottle over his head. The Question Box seemed to Ozma the most wonderful of all of Glegg's magic.

"Why, all we have to do is to ask this box questions," she cried in excitement. "Has my palace reached the Emerald City?" she asked breathlessly.

"Shake it three times," said Pompa, as Ozma looked in vain for her answer.

"Yes," stated the box after the third shake, and Ozma sighed with relief.

"I suppose you asked it if I were the Proper Princess mentioned in the scroll," she said, a bit shyly.

The Prince shook his head. "Knew without asking," said Pompa heavily.

"Do you mean to say you never asked it that?" gasped Ozma in disbelief. "Why, I am surprised at you." And before Pompa could object she shook the little box briskly. "Who is the Princess that Pompa must marry?" she demanded anxiously.

"The Princess of Sun Top Mountain," flashed the Question Box promptly. Then, as an afterthought, it added, "Trust the mirror and golden door knob!"

"Now, you see!" cried Ozma, jumping up in delight. "I wasn't the Proper Princess at all!"

Pompa smiled faintly, but without enthusiasm. The thought of hunting another Princess was almost too much. "I wish I could just take Peg Amy and Wag and go back to Pumperdink without marrying anybody," he choked bitterly.

"Now, don't give up," advised Ozma kindly. "It was very wrong of Glegg to cause you all this trouble. I'm going to keep his box of Mixed Magic and take away all his powers when I find him, but until I do, you'll have to follow directions. Oh mercy! What's that?"

They both ducked and turned around in a hurry, as a terrific thumping sounded behind them.

"It's the Runaway Country again," cried Pompa, seizing Ozma's hands in distress, "and it's caught all the others."

The Scarecrow had climbed a tree, and was waving to them wildly as the Country galloped nearer. "Might as well come aboard," he called genially. "This is a fast Country—no arguing with it at all."

Ozma looked helplessly at Pompa, and the Prince had only time to grasp her more firmly when the Country scooped them neatly into the air. Down they tumbled, beside Peg Amy and Wag and the Elegant Elephant.

"What do you mean by this?" demanded Ozma, as soon as she regained her breath.

"Don't you know this lady is the Ruler of all Oz?" cried Pompa warningly.

"Peg's the Ruler of me," replied the Country calmly. "I nearly lost her once, but now I've caught her and all the rest, and I am not going to stop until I've reached the Nonestic Ocean—giants or no giants."

Ozma had been somewhat prepared for the Runaway Country by Pompa's description, but she had never dreamed it would dare to run off with her. While Peg Amy began to coax it to stop, she took out Glegg's little Question Box.

"How shall I stop this Country?" she whispered anxiously.

"Spin around six times and cross your fingers," directed the Question Box.

This Ozma proceeded to do, much to the agitation of the Scarecrow, who thought she had taken leave of her senses. But next instant the Country came to a jolting halt.

"Peg, Princess Peg!" shrieked the Island. "I am bewitched, I can't move a step!"

"Then everybody off," shouted the Scarecrow, jerking a branch of a tree as if he were a conductor. "End of the line—everybody off!" And they lost no time tumbling off the wild little Country.

"It seems too bad to leave it," said Peg Amy regretfully, picking herself up.

"It threw us off without any feeling or consideration when it saw Ruggedo," sniffed Kabumpo. "Therefore it has no claims on us whatsoever."

"But couldn't you do something for it?" asked Peg, approaching Ozma timidly. "It's so tired of being a plateau. Couldn't you let it be an island, and find someone to settle on it? I wouldn't mind going," she added generously.

"You shall do nothing of the sort," cried Kabumpo angrily. "You're going back to Pumperdink with Pompa and me."

"She's going with me," cried Wag. "Aren't you, Peg?"

"You seem to be a very popular person," smiled Ozma. "While a Country has no right to run away, and while I never heard of one doing it before, I've no objections to its being an island. It's running off with people I object to." She looked the Country sternly in its lake-eyes.

"But I can't move," screamed the Country, tears streaming down its hill, "and I've got to have somebody to settle me."

"Oh! Here's Glinda," shouted the Scarecrow, tossing up his hat. "Now we shall know what's happened to Ruggedo."

Leaving the Country for a moment, they all ran to welcome the good Sorceress of Oz. Glinda's reports were most satisfactory. Ruggedo had walked straight back to the Emerald City, stepped into the yawning cavern, and immediately the palace had settled firmly upon its old foundations. Then had come a muffled explosion, and when Glinda and Dorothy ran through the secret passage, which had been discovered meanwhile by the Soldier with the Green Whiskers, they saw Ruggedo, shrunken to his former size, sitting angrily on his sixth rock of history.

"I have locked him up in the palace," finished Glinda, "and I strongly advise your Highness to punish him severely."

Ozma sighed. "What would you do?" she asked, appealing to the Scarecrow. So many things had come up for her attention and advice in the last few hours that the little fairy ruler felt positively dizzy.

"Let's all sit down in a circle and think," proposed the Scarecrow cheerfully. This they all did except Kabumpo, who stood off glumly by himself. Peg was looking anxiously at Pompadore, for the Elegant Elephant had told her of Ozma's refusal, and wondering sadly what she could do to help, when the Scarecrow bounced up impulsively.

"I have it," chuckled the Straw Man. "Let's send Ruggedo off on the Runaway Country. He deserves to be banished and, if Ozma makes the Country an Island, he can do no harm."

Here Ozma had to stop and explain to Glinda about the Country that wanted to be an Island, and after a short consultation they decided to take the Scarecrow's advice.

"Just as soon as I reach the Emerald City I'll put on my Magic Belt and wish him onto the Island," declared Ozma. "And I think we'd better go right straight back," she added thoughtfully, "for it's growing darker every minute and Dorothy will be anxious to hear everything that's happened."

"Now you"—Ozma tapped Pompadore gently on the arm—"You must start at once for Sun Top Mountain. I'm going to ask the Question Box just where it is."

Pompa sighed deeply, and when Ozma consulted the Question Box as to the location of Sun Top Mountain, it stated that this Kingdom was in the very Centre of the North Winkie Country. "That's fine," said Ozma, clapping her hands. "I'll have the Runaway country carry you over the Deadly Desert, and as soon as you have married the Princess you must bring her to see me in the Emerald City."

"Whats all this?" demanded Kabumpo, pricking up his ears.

"The Question Box says I must marry the Princess of Sun Top Mountain," said Pompa, getting up wearily.

"Well, Great Grump, why couldn't it have said so before?" asked Kabumpo shrilly.

"You never asked it," snapped Wag, twitching his nose. "I told you Ozma wasn't the Princess mentioned in the scroll!"

"Now don't quarrel," begged Peg Amy, jumping up hastily. "There's still plenty of time to save Pumperdink. Come along, Pompa."

"That's right," said Ozma, smiling approvingly at Peg. "And when Pompa finds his Princess you must come and live with me in the Emerald City, for as Ruggedo was responsible for bringing you to life, I want to take care of you always."

Peg Amy dropped a curtsey and promised to come, but she didn't feel very cheerful about it. Then, as Ozma was anxious to get back to the Emerald City, they all hurried to Runaway Country.

"You are to take these travelers across the Deadly Desert," said Ozma, addressing the Runaway Country quite sternly, "and you are to set them down in the Winkie Country. If you do this I will restore your moving power again and give you a little gnome for King. Then you may run off to the Nonestic Ocean as soon as ever you wish."

"I want Peg," pouted the Country, "but if that's the best you can do I suppose I'll have to stand it." After a little more grumbling it agreed to Ozma's terms. Wearily, Kabumpo, Wag, Peg and Pompa climbed aboard and then Ozma spun around six times in the opposite direction and immediately the Country found itself able to move again.

"Good-bye!" called Ozma, as she and the Scarecrow jumped into Glinda's chariot. "Good-bye and good luck!"

"Good-bye!" called Peg, waving her old torn bonnet.

"Good riddance," grumbled the Country gruffly and, turning sideways, began running toward the Deadly Desert.

Chapter 20
The Proper Princess Is Found!

"Is the mirror safe, and have you still got the gold door knob?" asked Pompa, as the Country swung out onto the Deadly Desert. "The Question Box said I was to trust them, you know."

"And by what right did Ozma take that box?" wheezed Kabumpo irritably, as he felt in his pocket to see whether the magic articles were still there.

"That's gratitude for you! We find Glegg's box of Mixed Magic and rescue her, and off she goes with all our magic, leaving us to the tender mercies of a Runaway Country!"

"You find the box!" shrilled Wag. "Well, I like that!"

"Oh, what difference does it make?" groaned Pompa, stretching out upon the ground. They were all completely exhausted by the day's adventures and as cross as three sticks—all except Peg Amy, who never was cross.

"I shall marry this Princess and save my country, but I'm going away as soon as the wedding is over and spend the rest of my life in travel," announced Pompa gloomily.

"Don't blame you," rumbled the Elegant Elephant with a sniff.

"Ah, now!" laughed Peg. "That doesn't sound like you, Pompa. Why, maybe this Princess will be so lovely you'll want to carry her straight back to Pumperdink."

"I think Princesses are a great bore," said Wag with a terrific yawn. "I prefer plain folks like Peg and the Scarecrow."

"You're all hungry, that's what's the matter," chuckled the Wooden Doll. "When you've had some supper you'll be just as anxious to find the Princess of Sun Top

Mountain as you were to find Ozma. Here's the Winkie Country now, and there's a star for good luck."

Peg waved toward the green fields with one hand and toward the clouds with the other. It was dusk now and just one star twinkled cheerily in the sky.

"I'll set you down, but I'm not going away," said the Runaway Country determinedly, "for if that little old gnome doesn't turn up I'm going to catch you all again."

"Ozma never forgets. She'll keep her promise," said Peg. "And you must do just as she told you to do for she has some powerful magic and can send you right back to where you came from."

"Can she?" gulped the Country anxiously.

"You might wait a while, though," suggested Pompa darkly. "After I've seen this new Princess a Runaway Country might be a very good thing."

"Well, you can't expect her to marry you if you talk that way," said Peg warningly, as the Country came to a stop in a huge field of daisies.

"I'll wait," it said hopefully, as the four travelers swung themselves down.

"I wonder if we are in the North Central part," murmured Peg Amy, looking around anxiously. Now it happened the Country had crossed the Deadly Desert slantwise and although none of the party knew it they were scarcely a mile from Sun Top Mountain.

"I see a garden!" cried Wag, twitching his nose hungrily. "Come on, Prince, lets find some supper." With head down and dragging his feet, Pompa followed Wag. Kabumpo began jerking snappishly at some tree tops and Peg Amy sat down to think.

"I wish," thought the Wooden Doll, looking up at the bright star, "I wish I might have asked the box one little question." Peg Amy looked so solemn that Kabumpo stopped eating and regarded her anxiously.

"What's the matter?" asked the Elegant Elephant gruffly, for he quite counted on Peg's cheerfulness.

"I was thinking about it again," admitted Peg apologetically. "About being alive before. I'm sure I was alive before I was a doll, Kabumpo. I think I was a person, like Pompa," she continued softly.

"You're much better as you are," said the Elegant Elephant uneasily, for it had just occurred to him that the Magic Mirror would tell Peg who she was as well as the Question Box. But should he let her look in it? That was the question. Poor, tired old Kabumpo shifted from one foot to the other as he tried to make up his mind. Two huge drops of perspiration ran down his trunk. What good would it do? he reasoned finally. Suppose it told something awful! It couldn't change her and it might make her unhappy. No, he would not let Peg look in the mirror.

"How would you like to have this pearl bracelet?" he asked in an embarrassed voice.

"Why, Kabumpo, I'd just adore it!" cried Peg, springing up in a hurry. "And I'm not going to worry about being alive any more, for everyone is so lovely to me I ought to be the happiest person in Oz."

"You are," puffed Kabumpo, clumsily slipping the bracelet on Peg's wooden arm, "and if we ever get back to Pumperdink you shall have as many silk dresses as you want and—" The rest of the sentence was smothered in a hug.

Peg Amy was growing fonder and fonder of pompous old Kabumpo and by the time he had recovered his breath Wag and the Prince came ambling back together. They had found an orchard and a kitchen garden and as they were no longer hungry, both were more cheerful.

"Let's play scop hotch," suggested Wag amiably. "I'm tired of hunting Princesses." There was a smooth patch of sand under the trees and Wag hopped over and began marking out the squares with his paw.

"Scop hotch!" laughed Pompa, While Peg gave a skip of delight.

"Play if you want to," wheezed Kabumpo, shaking himself wearily, "I feel about as playful as a stone lion. Besides, hop scotch isn't an elephant game."

Peg, Wag and Pompa began to hop scotch for dear life. Peg often tumbled over, for it is hard to keep your balance on wooden legs, but it was Peg who won in the end and Wag crowned her with daisies.

"I wish we could go on just as we are," gasped Pompa, mopping his face with his silk handkerchief. "We're all good chums and, if it weren't for Pumperdink's disappearing, we might travel all over Oz and have no end of adventures together."

"Speaking of disappearing," said Kabumpo, opening one eye, for he had dozed off during the game, "I suppose we'd better be starting if we're to save the Kingdom at all."

"Good-bye to pleasure," sighed Pompa, as Kabumpo lifted him to his back. "Good-bye to everything!"

"Oh, cheer up," begged Peg, settling herself on Wag's back.

"Hurrah! Hurrah! Hurrah!" A large yellow bird rose suddenly from a near-by bush and flapped its wings over Pompa's head. "Hurrah! Hurrah!"

"Shoo! Get away!" grumbled Kabumpo crossly. "What are you cheering about?"

"She said to," cawed the bird, darting over Peg Amy's head. "Hurrah! Hurrah! Hurrah! Let me teach you how to be cheerful in three chirps. First, think of what you might have been; next, think of what you are; then think of what you are going to be. Do you get it?" The bird put its head on one side and regarded them anxiously.

"He might have been King of Oz, instead of which he is only a lost Prince, and he's going to be married to a mountain top Princess. Do you see anything cheerful about that?" demanded Kabumpo angrily. "Clear out! We'll do our own cheering."

"Shall I go?" asked the Hurrah Bird, looking very crestfallen and pointing its claw at Peg Amy.

"Maybe you can tell us the way to Sun Top Mountain," said Peg politely.

"You can see it from the other side of the hill," replied the Hurrah Bird. "I'll give you a few hurrahs for luck. Hurrah! Hurrah! Hurrah!"

"Oh, go away," grumbled Kabumpo.

"Not till you look at my nest. Did you ever see a Hurrah Bird's nest?" he chirped brightly.

"Let's look at it," said Pompa, smiling in spite of himself. The Hurrah Bird preened itself proudly as they peered through the bushes. Surely it had the gayest nest ever built, for it was woven of straw of many colors, and hung all over the near-by branches were small Oz flags. In the nest three little yellow chicks were growing up into Hurrahs and they chirped faintly at the visitors.

"Remember," called the Father Hurrah, as they bade him good-bye, "you can always be cheerful in three chirps if you think of what you *might* have been, what you *are*, and what you are going to be. Hurrah! Hurrah! Hurrah!"

"There's something in what you've said," chuckled Wag. "Good-bye!"

The moon had come up brightly and even Kabumpo began to feel more like himself. "There's a lot to be learned by traveling, eh, Wag?" He winked at the rabbit, who was just behind him. "Let's see—somersaults for sums—never be gormish—and now, how to be cheerful in three chirps. Hurrah! Hurrah! Hurrah!" The Elegant Elephant began to plow swiftly through the daisy field, so that in almost no time they reached the top of the little hill and as they did so Peg gave a little scream of delight. As for the others, they were simply speechless.

A purple mountain rose steeply ahead, and set like a crown upon its summit was a glittering gold castle, the loveliest, laciest gold castle you could imagine, with a hundred fluttering pennants. All down the mountain side spread its lovely gardens, its golden arbors and flower bordered paths.

101

At the top of the mountain the loveliest castle you could imagine

"I've seen it before!" cried the Wooden Doll softly, but no one heard her. Pompa drew a deep breath, for the castle, shimmering in the moonlight, seemed almost too beautiful to believe.

"Whe-ew!" whistled Wag, breaking the silence. "The Princess of Tun Sop Wountain must be wonderful."

"Shall we start up now?" gasped Kabumpo, swinging his trunk nervously.

"I don't believe she'll ever marry me. Lets don't go at all," muttered the Prince of Pumperdink in a shaking voice.

"Oh, come on!" called Wag, who was curious to see the owner of so grand a castle.

"But we mustn't go, Wag," gasped Peg Amy. "How would it look to have a shabby old doll tagging along when he's trying to talk to the Princess?"

"If Peg doesn't go, I'm not going," declared Pompa stubbornly.

"You're just as good as any Princess," said Kabumpo, "and I'm not going without you, either."

As the Elegant Elephant refused to budge and there seemed no other way out of it, Peg Amy finally consented and the four adventurers started fearfully up the winding path, almost expecting the castle to disappear before they reached the top, so unreal did it seem in the moonlight. There was no one in the garden but there were lights in the castle windows. "Just as if they expected us," said the Elegant Elephant, as they reached the tall gates. Pompa opened the gates and next instant they were standing before the great castle door.

"Shall we knock?" chattered Wag, his eyes sticking out with excitement.

"No! Wait a minute," begged the Prince, who was becoming more agitated every minute.

"Here's the mirror and the door knob," quavered Kabumpo. "Didn't the Question Box say to trust them? Why, look here, Pompa, my boy, it fits!" Clumsily, Kabumpo held up the glittering door knob he had brought all the way from Pumperdink; then he slipped it easily on the small gold bar projecting from the door.

But instead of looking joyful Pompa groaned dismally. He started to protest but Kabumpo had already turned the knob and they found themselves in a glittering gold court room.

"Now for the Princess," puffed Kabumpo, looking around with his twinkling little eyes. "Here, take the mirror, Pompa." The room was empty, although brilliantly lighted, and the Prince stood uncertainly in the very center. Suddenly, with a determined little cry, Pompa rushed over to Peg Amy, who stood leaning against a tall gold chair.

"Peg," choked Pompa, dropping on his knees beside the Wooden Doll, "I'll have to find some other way to save Pumperdink. I'm not going to marry this Princess and have you taken away from me. You're a proper enough Princess for me and we'll just go back to Pumperdink and be—"

"The mirror! Look in the mirror!" screamed Wag, who was sitting beside Peg Amy.

There stood Peg Amy, the Loveliest Little Princess in the world

Unconsciously, Pompa had held out the gold mirror and Peg, leaning over to listen, had looked directly into it. Above Peg's pleasant reflection in the mirror they read these startling and important words:

This is Peg Amy, Princess of Sun Top Mountain.

While Pompa stared with round eyes the words faded out and this new legend formed in the glass:

This is the Proper Princess.

"I always knew you were a Princess," cried Wag, turning a somersault.

The big rabbit had just come right-side-up, when a still more amazing thing happened. The wooden body of Peg melted before their eyes and in its place stood the loveliest little Princess in the world. And yet, with all her beauty, she was strangely like the old Peg. Her eyes had the same merry twinkle and her mouth the same pleasant curve.

"Oh!" cried Princess Peg, holding her arms out to her friends. "Now I am the happiest person in Oz!"

Chapter 21
How It All Came About

Before Pompa had time to rise, a tall, richly clad old nobleman rushed into the room. "Peg!" cried the old gentleman, clasping the Princess in his arms. "You are back! At last the enchantment is broken!"

For a moment the two forgot all about Pompa and the others. Then, gently disengaging herself, Peg seized the Prince's hands and drew him to his feet.

"Uncle," she said breathlessly, holding to Pompa with one hand and waving with the other at Kabumpo and Wag, "here are the friends responsible for my release. This is my Uncle Tozzyfog," she explained quickly, and impulsively Uncle Tozzyfog sprang to his feet and embraced each in turn—even Kabumpo.

"Sit down," begged the old nobleman, sinking into a golden chair and mopping his head with a flowered silk kerchief.

Pompa, who could not take his eyes from this new and wonderful Peg Amy, dropped into another chair. Kabumpo leaned limply against a pillar and Wag sat where he was, his nose twitching faster than ever and his ears stuck out straight behind him.

"You are probably wondering about the change in Peg," began Uncle Tozzyfog, as the Princess perched on the arm of his chair, "so I'll try to tell my part of the story. Three years ago an ugly old peddlar climbed the path to Sun Top Mountain. He said his name was Glegg and, forcing his way into the castle, he demanded the hand of my niece in marriage."

Peg shuddered and Uncle Tozzyfog blew his nose violently at the distressing memory. Then, speaking rapidly and pausing every few minutes to appeal to the Princess, he continued the story of Peg's enchantment. Naturally the old peddlar had been refused and thrown out of the castle. That night as Uncle Tozzyfog prepared to carve the royal roast, there came an explosion, and when the Courtiers had picked themselves up Peg Amy was nowhere to be seen, and only a threatening scroll remained to explain the mystery. Glegg, who was really a powerful magician, infuriated by Uncle Tozzyfog's treatment, had changed the little Princess into a tree.

"Know ye," began the scroll quite like the one that had spoiled Pompa's birthday, "know ye that unless ye Princess of Sun Top Mountain consents to wed J. Glegg she shall remain a tree forever, or until two shall call and believe her to be a Princess. J. G."

The whole castle had been plunged into utmost gloom by this terrible happening, for Peg was the kindliest, best loved little Princess any Kingdom could wish for. Lord Tozzyfog and nearly all the Courtiers set out at once to search for the little tree and for two years they wandered over Oz, addressing every hopeful tree as Princess, but never happening on the right one. Finally they returned in despair and Sun Top Mountain, once the most cheerful Kingdom in all Oz, had become the gloomiest. There was no singing, nor dancing—no happiness of any kind. Even the flowers had drooped in the absence of their little Mistress.

"Why didn't you appeal to Ozma?" demanded Pompa at this point in the story.

"Because in another scroll Glegg warned us that the day we told Ozma, Peg Amy would cease to even be a tree," explained Uncle Tozzyfog hoarsely.

"Then how did she become a doll? Tell me that, Uncle Fozzytog," gulped Wag, raising one paw.

"She'll have to tell you that herself," confessed Peg's uncle, "for that's all of the story I know."

So here Peg took up the story herself. The morning after her transformation into a tree Glegg had appeared and asked her again to marry him. "I was a little yellow tree, in the Winkie Country, not far from the Emerald City," explained Peg, "and every day for two months Glegg appeared and gave me the power of speech long enough to answer his question. And each time he asked me to marry him but I always said 'No!'" The Princess shook her yellow curls briskly.

"Every day Glegg returned and asked me to marry him, but I always said 'No'!" explained Peg "One afternoon there came a one-legged sailor man and a little girl." Even Kabumpo shuddered as Peg Amy told how Cap'n Bill had cut down the little tree, pared off all the branches and carved from the trunk a small wooden doll for Trot.

"It didn't hurt," Princess Peg hastened to explain as she caught Pompa's sorrowful expression, "and being a doll was a lot better than being a tree. I could not move or speak but I knew what was going on and life in Ozma's palace was cheerful and interesting. Only, of course, I longed to tell Ozma or Trot of my enchantment. I missed dear Uncle Tozzyfog and all the people of Sun Top Mountain. Then, as you all know, I was stolen by the old gnome and after Ruggedo carried me underground I forgot all about being a Princess and remembered nothing of this." Peg glanced lovingly around the room. "I only felt that I had been alive before. So you!" Peg jumped up and flung one arm around Wag, "and you," she flung the other around Pompa, "saved me by calling me a Princess and really believing I was one. And you!" Peg hastened over to Kabumpo, who was rolling his eyes sadly. "You are the darlingest old elephant in Oz! See, I still have the necklace and bracelet!" And sure enough on Peg's round arm and white neck gleamed the jewels the Elegant Elephant had generously given when he thought her only a funny Wooden Doll.

"Oh!" groaned Kabumpo. "Why didn't I let you look in the mirror before? No wonder you kept remembering things."

"But why did Glegg send the threatening scroll to Pumperdink three years after he'd enchanted Peg?" asked Wag, scratching his head.

"Because!" shrilled a piercing voice, and in through the window bounded a perfectly dreadful old man. It was Glegg himself!

"In through the window bounded a perfectly dreadful old man"

"Because!" screeched the wicked magician, advancing toward the little party with crooked finger, "when that meddling old sailor touched Peg with his knife I lost all power over her; because my Question Box told me that Pompadore of Pumperdink could bring about her disenchantment and he has. I made it interesting for you, didn't I? There isn't another magician in Oz can put scrolls up in cakes and roasts

105

like I can nor mix magic like mine. Ha! Ha!" Glegg threw back his head and rocked with enjoyment. "You have had all the trouble and I shall have all the reward!"

Everyone was so stunned by this terrible interruption that no one made a move as Glegg sprang toward Peg Amy. But before he had reached the Princess there was a queer sulphurous explosion and the magician disappeared in a cloud of green smoke. They rubbed their eyes and as the smoke cleared they saw Trot, the little girl who had played with Peg Amy when she was a Wooden Doll.

"Ozma," explained Trot breathlessly, for she had come on a fast *wish*.

After following the adventures of Pompa and Peg in the Magic Mirror, and as the magician had tried to snatch the Princess, Ozma had transported him by means of her Magic Belt to the Emerald City, and sent Trot to bring her best wishes to the whole party.

"I'm sorry I didn't make you a prettier dress when you were my doll," said Trot, seizing Peg Amy's hand impulsively, "but you see I didn't know you were a Princess."

"But you guessed my name," said Peg softly.

There were so many explanations to be made and so many things to wonder over and exclaim about, that it seemed as if they could never stop talking.

Uncle Tozzyfog rang all the bells in the castle tower and stepping out on a balcony told the people of Sun Top Mountain of the return of Princess Peg Amy. Then the servants were summoned and such a feast as only an Oz cook can prepare was started in the castle kitchen. The Courtiers came hurrying back, for during Peg's absence Uncle Tozzyfog had lived alone in the castle. Yes, the Courtiers came back and the people of Sun Top Mountain poured into the castle in throngs and nearly overwhelmed the rescuers by the enthusiasm of their thanks.

Kabumpo had never been so admired and complimented in his whole elegant life. As for Wag, his speech grew more mixed up every minute. At last, when the Courtiers and Uncle Tozzyfog had run off to dress for the grand banquet, and after Trot had been magically recalled by Ozma to the Emerald City, the four who had gone through so many adventures together were left alone.

"Well, how about Pumperdink, my boy?" chuckled Kabumpo, with a wave of his trunk. "Are we going to let the old Kingdom disappear or not?"

"It is my duty to save my country," said Pompa loftily. Then, with a mischievous smile at Peg Amy, "Don't you think so, Princess?" Peg Amy looked merrily at the Elegant Elephant and then took Pompa's hand.

"Yes, I do," said the Princess of Sun Top Mountain.

"Then, you *will* marry me?" asked Pompa, looking every inch a Prince in spite of his singed head and torn clothes.

"We must save Pumperdink, you know," sighed Peg softly.

"Three cheers for the Princess of Pumperdink! May she be as happy as the day is short!" cried Wag in his impulsive way.

Uncle Tozzyfog was as pleased as Wag when he heard the news, and Pompa, attired in a royal gold embroidered robe, was married to Peg Amy upon the spot, with much pomp and magnificence.

Never before was there such rejoicing—a merrier company or a happier bride. Kabumpo, arrayed in two gold curtains borrowed for the happy occasion, had never appeared more elegant and Wag was everywhere at once and simply overwhelmed with attention.

That same night a messenger was dispatched to Pumperdink to carry the good news and the next morning Pompa and Peg set out for the Emerald City, the Princess riding proudly on Wag and Pompadore on Kabumpo. Knowing the whole four as you now do, you will believe me when I say that their journey was the merriest and most delightful ever recorded in the merry Kingdom of Oz.

After a short visit with Ozma and another to the King and Queen of Pumperdink they all returned to Sun Top Mountain, where they are living happily at this very minute.

Chapter 22
Ruggedo's Last Rock

There are only a few more mysteries to clear up before we leave for a time the jolly Kingdom of Oz. Ruggedo, much shaken by his terrible experiences with Glegg's magic, confessed everything to Ozma on her return to the Emerald City. You can imagine the surprise of the little Fairy Ruler on learning how her palace had come to be impaled upon the spikes of the wicked old gnome's gray head.

"He will nev-er re-form," said Tik Tok mournfully, as Ruggedo finished his recital. The bad little gnome assured Ozma that he had reformed and begged for another chance, but this time Ozma knew better, and putting on her Magic Belt she whispered a few secret words. Then they all hurried over to the Magic Picture, for they knew that Ruggedo had been transported to a safe place at last. The picture showed the Runaway Country rushing along faster than an express train and dancing up and down on its highest hill was the furious old King of the Gnomes. They watched until the Country plunged joyfully into the Nonestic Ocean and, when it was almost in the middle, Ozma stopped it by the magic spinning process and it became Ruggedo's Island.

"Well," sighed Dorothy as they turned from the picture, "I guess that will be Ruggedo's last rock!"

"He's rocked in the cradle of the deep now," chuckled the Scarecrow. "And I hope it quiets him down. They ought to make a good pair—that bad little Island and that bad little King," he added reflectively.

"I guess that will be Ruggedo's last rock," said Dorothy

Then Ozma proposed that they follow the adventures of Peg and Pompa, having so satisfactorily disposed of Ruggedo. How she transported Glegg just in time to save the Princess you already know. But what happened to Glegg himself is interesting. When the old magician had asked his Question Box how to regain control over Peg again it had directed him to bury his Mixed Magic under the Emerald City and in two years to send the scroll to Pumperdink. So Glegg had tunneled out the cave under Ozma's palace and left his magic in what he supposed was a very safe place. It had been a great hardship to do without it for two years, but he wanted Peg so badly that he actually did this, never dreaming that Ruggedo had moved in and discovered his treasures. The Question Box had told the exact day Peg would be disenchanted and all that long two years Glegg had waited, hidden in a forest near Sun Top Mountain.

As he knew nothing of the discovery of his magic box, no one was more surprised than he to find himself, just as he was on the point of seizing Peg, transported to the Emerald City.

While Sir Hokus of Pokes held the struggling Glegg, Ozma asked the Question Box how to deal with him. Everybody crowded around the little Fairy Ruler to hear what the wicked old magician's fate was to be.

"Give him a taste of his own magic," directed the Question Box. "Make him drink a cup of his Triple Trick Tea." This Ozma did, although it took fourteen people to get Glegg to drink it. But, stars! No sooner had the liquid touched his lips than the miserable old magician went off with a loud explosion!

The box of Mixed Magic was carefully put away in Ozma's gold safe and then the whole company—Ozma, Dorothy, Sir Hokus, the Scarecrow and all the celebrities—devoted themselves to setting the topsy turvy palace to rights, for they knew by the Magic picture that Pompa and Peg Amy were coming to visit them.

"Glegg, Glegg, shake a leg
And never more, Sir, bother Peg!"
shouted Scraps, as she swept up the black soot Glegg had left when he exploded. And he never did.

Note from the Editor

Odin's Library Classics strives to bring you unedited and unabridged works of classical literature. As such this is the complete and unabridged version of the original English text. The English language has evolved since the writing and some of the words appear in their original form, or at least the most commonly used form at the time. This is done to protect the original intent of the author. If at any time you are unsure of the meaning of a word, please do your research on the etymology of that word. It is important to preserve the history of the English language.

Taylor Anderson

Printed in Great Britain
by Amazon